She would have stumbled into the brook except that the duke had reached her and, without a word, caught her up in his arms. She stared at him, speechless, and he still said nothing, merely looking down at her intently for a moment before he bent his black head to her. His mouth was warm and alive, and what began as a tender kiss soon deepened in passion, and although she felt faint and breathless, she didn't want him to stop.

Finally, the duke set her on the ground. "Breathless, m'lady? Well, I have carried out instructions, and it appears to have won the trick!"

KATHLEEN

Barbara Hazard

FAWCETT CREST • NEW YORK

A Fawcett Crest Book
Published by Ballantine Books
Copyright © 1980 by Barbara Hazard

ISBN 0-449-21250-5

Manufactured in the United States of America

First Fawcett Crest Edition: March 1980
First Ballantine Books Edition: October 1986

THIS BOOK IS DEDICATED
TO MY MOTHER WITH LOVE
. . . AND IN FOND MEMORY OF
MY FATHER

CHAPTER I

(Enter Our Hero and Heroine)

The two gentlemen from London trotted down the dusty road at a leisurely pace. Ireland in the late spring was a thousand shades of green, complimented by the blue of the sky above. Their way led them past rolling fields, down country lanes alive with bird-song and wild roses, through small villages and past lonely crofts. It was a perfect morning for a ride, but one of them at least did not appear to notice the scenery; in fact, there was a distinct frown on his handsome, bored face. This gentleman looked like he had been riding high-spirited horses since childhood, and although his riding clothes were dusty from the traveling, they proclaimed a master tailor, so beautifully were they molded to his large, masculine frame. His companion appeared to be the younger of the pair; he was a slighter man with a cheerful mien, as if he were more in the habit of smiling than frowning, and as if he had found life to be more merry than unsatisfactory. Now, as they crested a small rise, he glanced at his traveling companion and burst into laughter.

"Giles!" he exclaimed. "Devil take it, man, you look as if the weight of the world were riding on your shoulders! What an unhappy expression! Were you thinking of estate problems? Gambling debts? Perhaps a lady who is not succumbing to your masculine blandishments? No, it can't be any of those. Your estate was in excellent order when we left it last week, you're too wealthy to worry about debts, even if you didn't have the devil's own luck at the tables, and every woman I've ever seen has all but swooned if you but look her way with interest. What can it be, then?"

His companion curled his lip and raised one mobile black eyebrow.

"Can that be jealousy I hear in your voice, dear cousin? And yet, you are not exactly poverty-stricken, ugly, or unlucky yourself!"

"No, but compared to the Duke of Havenhall I am quite cast in the shade, and well I know it! Come, Giles, what's troubling you?"

The duke stared down the road pensively.

"Why, my dear Robert, I was merely thinking that if I had known you meant to travel from one end of this benighted island to the other, I would never have agreed to accompany you. Certainly 'tis a long and wearisome trip just to see a few horses! No," he said, raising one long, thin hand as his cousin attempted to speak, "say not a word. We are here, heaven knows where, and eventually we will arrive at our destination, before the season opens in London next year, I hope. Let me tell you, though, Cousin, these thoroughbreds of yours had really better be something quite out of common, or I will have something to say to you!"

"But Giles," Robert protested hotly, "you know that matched pair that Lord Ramsdale won from Sir Percy at White's was purchased at Evelon, and you said yourself they were superior stock. I thought you would be glad to get a march on the rest of the Four Horse Club, to say nothing of his lordship. You are not exactly the best of friends, as I recall."

If Robert had been watching more carefully, he would have seen Giles' hands tighten imperceptibly on the reins. He did, however, observe the sudden gleam from his dark eyes before the drooping lids almost hid them from view.

"Why, Robert," the duke drawled, "how can you say so? I pray you won't tell me that someone has accused me of incivility toward Lord Ramsdale? As you know, we meet frequently in London, and I had prided myself on my courtesy to him."

His cousin laughed nervously. The duke's tone had seemed almost icy—and very ducal.

"Of course not, Giles," he reassured him. "'Tis only my own observation. You are all that is correct, but perhaps there is in your manner some hint of coldness? I have often wished I knew what had occurred between you to cause this."

Giles glanced at him and smiled slightly.

"Well, m'dear, who knows? Perhaps someday I'll tell you, but for now I wish you would tell *me* how much farther we have to ride to this distant farm?"

"Well, the innkeeper did not say it was too far. As I recall, he mentioned merely a pleasant ride . . ."

"My dear Robert! Surely you know by now that asking directions in the country will rarely get you an accurate answer! For all we know, his 'pleasant ride' could continue for hours more!"

"Nay, Giles," Robert protested, "for you yourself ordered a neat dinner on our return, and surely he would have said something if the distance were too far for us to return in time."

The two gentlemen continued their ride, and in truth, it was not many more minutes before they perceived a gatehouse and drive ahead. The gatekeeper assured them that it was indeed Evelon Farm, and Giles sighed in relief to tease Robert one more time as they urged their horses on.

On either side of the drive they were traveling, the lush spring fields of Evelon Farm stretched in every direction. They could see mares and colts in some of the fields, and ahead of them there was a large farmhouse, which Giles thought was probably considered a manor house here. Glancing idly about, Robert suddenly exclaimed,

"Giles! Look there! In that distant field! Did you ever see such horseflesh?"

Giles followed his pointing crop. A large black stallion was just taking a fence, and he was a beautiful sight. His rider urged him on at even greater pace, and he galloped out of sight behind a small hill.

"There now, Giles! Even you must admit that an animal like that is worth a trip to Ireland! What a beauty! I wonder if he is for sale?"

They drew rein in front of the farmhouse and leisurely dismounted. A boy hurried from the stables to attend their horses, and from the front door appeared a large man wiping his face with a napkin. They had obviously interrupted a late breakfast or an early nuncheon. Giles moved unhurriedly toward the steps. Now he was standing, it could be seen that he was well over six feet in height with magnificent shoulders and long, powerful legs. No London fop here, despite his stylish clothes; his every movement proclaimed the athlete. His face appeared bored until he smiled, and then even the most exacting critics would say he was handsome. Unfortunately, he smiled seldom.

The red-faced gentleman reached the bottom of the steps, thrusting the napkin into his hacking jacket. He was dressed for riding and appeared to be about fifty years old, with a ruddy complexion, a large stomach, and a head of flaming red hair dusted with white at the temples.

"Good day to you, gentlemen! And what can we be doing for you at Evelon? I'm Malloy, you know," he continued, holding out a large hand in welcome.

"And I am Giles Brentwood, and this is my cousin, Robert Marlow."

As they exchanged handshakes, the Irishman inquired shrewdly, "Ah, would that be the Giles Brentwood, duke of Havenhall?"

The duke's eyebrows ascended in surprise, but Robert laughed at him and chided, "Why Giles! Your fame proceeds you! Even in Ireland they know your name!"

Lord Malloy hastened to make things clearer.

"Your Grace, 'tis only that I have spent some time in England in my youth, and my wife, though long since departed, was Lady Evelyn Montgomery of Greywood. But come, what am I thinking of, to keep you standing here on the steps? Please come inside—perhaps a bite to eat after your long ride would not be amiss. At least join me in a tankard of ale while you tell me how I may serve you."

So saying, he ushered them into a low-ceilinged, dimly lit hall. At one end there was a large fireplace with a cheerful blaze taking off the morning chill. Several hounds dozed before the fire. Looking around, Giles could see several mismatched chairs, and in the center of the hall a large table on which rested crops, riding gloves, a broken pistol, and assorted odds and ends. It was obvious Lord Malloy's wife had departed this life, for he knew that no woman would have put up with the clutter.

Their host led them to a room at the back of the hall and shouted for a servant. This room was bright with sunlight, and several people had finished breakfast from the looks of the settings which had not been cleared away.

"Katie Mary!" Lord Malloy called. "Katie Mary! Where the devil is the girl?"

"You forget, sir," the servant who was bustling in said. "Lady Kathleen Mary is riding Diablo this morning and has not returned."

"Sure, and of course, my wits have gone begging!" He turned to his two guests. "'Tis my daughter—how could I forget? She rides that stallion every morning, for she prefers to see to his exercise herself. She should soon return. In the meantime, what can we get you for refreshment? Some of this sirloin? A bit of ham, perhaps?"

"Nothing, sir, I thank you, except for a tankard of ale. 'Tis a fair ride from the village, and we are parched," Giles replied.

As the servant hastened to serve them, Robert inquired eagerly, "Is this stallion you speak of perhaps the one we saw while we were riding in? A large black horse, the most magnificent animal!"

"Aye, that would be Diablo, especially if he was being ridden hell for leather," Lord Malloy chuckled.

"Well, I tell you frankly, sir," Robert continued, "we are here to look over your stables. We have heard many things about your horses, but I doubt there are any more splendid than that black stallion. Is he perchance for sale?"

Giles lounged back in his chair, a small smile on his lips. Robert had a long way to go to become a successful horse trader. Such eagerness would never get him a bargain!

"My boy, I could never sell that horse. To be truthful with you, 'tis not mine to sell. My daughter fell in love with him as a colt, and I gave him to her. He has sired many beautiful colts though, we keep him at stud. Perhaps if you have finished your ale you would care to see some of his progeny? I warrant you won't be disappointed in his offspring!"

He led them back to the hall, which now seemed overly full of large young men who at first glance appeared to be trying their best to dispose of each other.

"Here, Michael! Anthony! George! Whatever will the gentlemen think? Stop this foolery at once! And where are Andrew and John?"

The wrestlers broke apart laughing. They were all as redheaded as their father, and all so large that three of them appeared to be at least six.

"Father, Andrew has ridden to the village with the bridle you wanted mended, and John is with Matthews watching over Gray Lady—she is foaling this morning," one of the boys replied.

As introductions were performed, Giles murmured an aside to Robert, "One need not ask why Lady Malloy succumbed early in life. Six children that we have heard of, and one assumes each larger than the next!"

Robert stifled a laugh as they descended the steps.

The muffled gallop of a horse was heard, and as one man they turned in that direction in time to see the black stallion come cantering up the drive to be reined in at their feet. Giles inspected him carefully as he pawed the ground and tossed his head as if he knew he were on center stage. He *was* a magnificent animal. His rider slid to the ground without help, and Giles looked around, his attention caught by a muffled exclamation from Robert. Surely *this* was a magnificent animal too, the Lady Kathleen Mary, no doubt. She had been riding astride in men's breeches which did nothing to hide her long slim legs and slender waist. A mother would have told her that she had outgrown the white lawn-shirt she wore. Her breasts strained against the lace. Her face was tanned but altogether lovely, from her sparkling blue eyes and her short, straight nose, to her full lips that seemed made to be kissed. Her chestnut hair, a shade darker than her father's, was pulled back carelessly and caught up behind with a thong. She was completely unself-conscious and gave each of the strangers a smile as her father introduced her proudly. She handed the reins to a waiting stable boy and removed a riding glove from one slim hand and shook hands with both Giles and Robert. Robert stammered a bit, he had to look up at her slightly she was so tall, and as he spoke, a dimple quivered beside her full mouth. Giles was amused. Another conquest for the lady, although she did not seem to care. She strolled with them to the stables, and he was struck with her long stride, so free in her boy's breeches. She also took full part in the conversation—at one point correcting her father about some colt they were about to see. She was obviously well schooled in the working of the farm and knew each of the horses intimately.

As they approached the nearest stable, a redheaded boy ran out of a neighboring barn and called anxiously, "Katie Mary! Come quickly! Gray Lady is about to drop her foal, and Matthews needs you."

Without a word of excuse, she whirled and ran to the barn. Giles enjoyed every stride. She even ran like a boy, but there was no mistaking her, even from the back, for a stripling. Robert appeared to be struck dumb.

After admiring several horses and discussing the fine points of some promising colts, both gentlemen were agreed that there were several animals well worth their time and pocketbooks. Lord Malloy left them near the stables, admiring a dapple colt, while he went back to the house to order some refreshments to be ready after the business at hand was concluded. Giles leaned idly on the corral fence.

"Isn't she beautiful, Giles?"

"That colt?" he said, looking more carefully at the dapple. "Well, frankly I think we have seen better this morning, although I will admit that you were right to insist we come here, tiring as it has been. When one thinks of the return voyage, one can but shudder . . ."

"No, no, Giles! Not the horse! The Lady Kathleen Mary! Have you ever seen such a face and figure? And that hair! Even you must admit she is something out of the common way!"

"Yes, I suppose so," Giles replied casually. "A veritable *nonpareil* in fact." His tone was carefully nonchalant. It was really so easy to tease Robert, he rose to every bait.

"Can't you just imagine her in London? Surely when she entered a ballroom, all heads would turn and complete silence fall before such beauty!" Robert continued enthusiastically.

"Now there you are wrong, Robert. Silence would fall and heads would turn, but I assure you 'twould be merely because of the lady's size, and her mannish stride. Lud, the Beau would have a fine time with her. Can't you just imagine his comments?" Giles chuckled at the thought.

Robert interrupted hotly. "How can you say so, Giles? Such beauty, such perfection! She must surely be admired!"

"I am sure she is admired here—she is perfect for her setting, there I do agree with you. One can only be sorry for her, however, that her mother did not live long enough to teach her the things a lady should know. She

has obviously been brought up as one of the
sons of the house, in fact, her father seems to
depend on her knowledge of the horses and the
farm a great deal. You can tell from the manor
that a woman's touch is absent. One can only
imagine she will remain here, marrying some
hearty farmer or squire, and probably produc-
ing as many children as her mother. But gay
repartie, the newest fashion, the latest
dance . . . no, definitely not her *métier*."

The two gentlemen wandered toward the
house, Robert still vehemently protesting, Giles
still gently disagreeing.

On the other side of the stable wall near
where they had been standing, the Lady Kathleen Mary, her blue eyes blazing, took a deep
breath. She had heard the entire conversation,
and her mood, which had been pleased to begin
with, had swiftly turned to anger and chagrin.
How dare he! That London fop to talk about
her that way! Perfect for her setting, indeed!
As she recalled some of Giles' other comments,
her anger rose. Marry some hearty farmer! A
blush rose to her cheeks as she recalled Tom
Gilroy, who had been following her around for
years, his heart written on his face for all the
world to see. Tom certainly was hearty, all
fifteen stone of him! And she herself had even
considered that some day, when Father and the
boys didn't need her any more, she
might . . . and mannish stride! Well! Did he
expect her to mince about the stable yard,
fainting at the sight of a bee! She glanced

down at her bloody apron. Gray Lady had foaled, another beauty too, but she had needed help. She should have marched out there (with her mannish stride) just as she was. The grand duke would probably have been overcome by the sight.

All the time she was cleaning up, she raged at the gentleman from London. Oh, what she'd give to show him! Dreamily drying her hands, she tried to imagine a London ballroom, herself in a glimmering gown of satin and lace, cutting him dead when he approached to beg her for a dance. Suddenly her anger melted, and her ever-ready good humor came to her rescue. Aye, that would be something, wouldn't it, my girl? You'd probably pop a seam, you don't know how to curtsy, and you can't dance! It certainly was maddening to admit he was right, especially since she had felt a distinct attraction to him when they were introduced. Her heart had given the oddest little jump when he took her hand and smiled down at her.

She hurried up to the house and entered a side door. She knew she couldn't meet either gentleman again and contain herself. She gave orders in the kitchen to the housekeeper and retired to her room, feigning an unusual headache if her father should inquire for her. And inquire he did when the men got down to the business at hand. She could hear him calling for her from where she waited behind her bedroom door. The housekeeper, Mrs. Keever, explained the headache, much to the disap-

pointment of her father, who liked Kathleen
Mary's quick wits about him in business trans-
actions, and who had to make do with his
oldest son Michael, and Robert, who had been
eagerly waiting for another glance at the lady,
no matter what Giles said.

The business was concluded to everyone's
satisfaction. Giles purchased a pair of matched
grays for his curricle, and two saddle horses,
while Robert bought a black horse Lord Malloy
assured him was a bruiser in the hunting field.
When Mrs. Keever brought light refreshments,
Robert left Giles talking desultorily with Michael and sought Lord Malloy's side. He wished
to know more about Kathleen Mary.

"I say, sir," he began, "your late wife's name
seems very familiar to me. I have heard my
mother mention Lady Evelyn. Would she have
been connected with the Montgomerys of
Hertfordshire by any chance?"

Lord Malloy sighed heavily.

"Aye, that she was. Of course, none of the
family would so much as mention her name
again after she eloped with a penniless Irish
earl down to London to see the sights. It was
a case of love at first sight . . ." He mopped his
suddenly damp eyes, and Robert glanced at
Giles for support. Giles didn't appear to notice
his predicament, damn him!

"Yes," Lord Malloy continued, "we married
at Gretna and my lady declared she was never
sorry, so happy as we were! Kathleen Mary is
the spitting image of her mother at that age."

"Then you were indeed fortunate," Robert interposed smoothly, "for I have never seen the Lady Kathleen Mary's equal. She would take London by storm if she were ever to appear!"

Lord Malloy brightened at the compliment to his only daughter.

"Aye, you've the right of it, sir! She is a beauty, but as for appearing in London, it has never been thought on. Her grandmother would never receive her, and if her mother's family will not support her, how can she make her come-out? No, she is happy here, and I myself do not know what I would do without her."

Eventually shipment for the horses they had purchased had been arranged, and Giles and Robert mounted their horses for the long ride back to the inn where they were staying until their departure from Ireland on the morrow. Robert was thwarted of another sight of the lady, for she remained discreetly in her room. If Giles was aware of a pair of angry blue eyes piercing his back as they rode down the avenue, he made no mention of it.

CHAPTER II

(Our Angry Heroine Contrives)

In the days that followed, Kathleen Mary appeared to be slightly absent-minded. Her brothers twitted her when she had to be spoken to twice, and didn't appear to be listening to the conversation at the dinner table. The twins, Anthony and George, who were now twenty years old to her eighteen, accused her of falling in love with the huge Tom; surely, they pointed out, that was the only thing that could account for her behavior. The younger boys collapsed with laughter at the thought, but then, at twelve and fourteen, being in love was most certainly amusing.

One evening, Kathleen Mary sought out her father as he sat in the estate room, checking some books.

"Father, may I speak to you?" she inquired from the door.

Lord Malloy brightened. Anything that kept him from his accounts was a welcome diversion, and his lovely daughter could always cheer him.

"Come in, my dear, and what can I be doing

for you this fine evening? 'Tis no problem at the stables, is it?"

"No, Father, the problem has nothing to do with the stables, for once," she replied, coming in and settling down in a comfortable old armchair near his desk. "The problem is me, I'm afraid."

He looked at her closely and once again wished for his wife's presence. It was no easy matter to raise a daughter alone. Uneasily, he waited while she fidgeted with the sash of her dress. At last she sighed and looked up at him.

"Father, I would like to go to London."

"What? Go to London?" he exclaimed. "And may I ask why, miss?"

"Well, it's difficult to explain, Father, but it has occurred to me that I am eighteen years old and I have never been anywhere. I would like to see something of the world before I am old . . ."

Lord Malloy smiled at her tenderly.

"Why, Katie Mary, you've years before you're old! And what would you do in London? And who would you stay with?"

She gave him a sideways glance. This was the hard part.

"Father, you know I have a little money from Mother. I would like to use that to buy some pretty clothes, and for traveling. As to staying in London, I thought if I perhaps wrote to my grandmother, she might be kind enough to sponsor me."

"What?" he bellowed. "Sponsor you? She's

not had a crumb to do with any of us in twenty-five years, as well you know. Sponsor you, indeed! You'd get short shrift from that old Tartar, my girl!''

Kathleen Mary leaned toward him eagerly.

"But Da," she said, using her baby name for him, "couldn't I try? If, as you say, she refuses to see me, then that's the end of it, but if she says yes, I would so much like to go!''

Lord Malloy sighed. He knew he was never able to resist his daughter; he was only sorry she was going to be disappointed. Well he remembered the confrontation with his wife's mother when they had returned from their hasty marriage. She had all but had him thrown from the house on Eaton Square, and what she had said to him alone could still raise a shiver on the back of his ruddy neck. He put from his mind how he and the boys would manage if Kathleen Mary were away for a lengthy stay, there was very little chance of that. Suddenly he remembered Robert Marlow's enthusiasm for his daughter.

"And what brought this about, Katie?" he asked. "Could it be that the fine gentlemen from London caught your eye? They're not for the likes of you. Be happy, and marry Tom Gilroy, and don't go chasing after London swells like that!''

Lord Malloy was not to know he had hit the nail on the head. Kathleen Mary flushed angrily.

"I wouldn't give him the time of day,

Father!" she exclaimed. "Conceited idiot! Whatever are you thinking? I'm sure I have better taste than that! But oh, I wish I could see London before I settle down with Tom or any other man!"

Lord Malloy had missed her reference to "one" gentleman in particular for he was thinking hard. At last he said,

"Well, then, m'darling, write to your grandmother if you wish. You have my permission for a visit, if it should work out, but Katie"—as she jumped to her feet and rushed to hug him—"don't be too disappointed if her answer is no, or even if she doesn't answer at all. You know she has never forgiven your mother for throwing herself away on an Irishman when she had a duke all picked out for her."

Kathleen Mary assured her father she would not be disappointed and soon took her leave of him in order to hurry to her room to begin composing a letter that would surely make Lady Montgomery all anxiety to see her only granddaughter.

Her absent-mindedness of the past few days had indeed been the result of the visit of Giles and Robert. At first she had been too angry with what she had heard in the stable to do more than rage inwardly whenever she thought of it, and that was often. Several times a day she caught herself thinking "how dare he?" or "and another thing . . ."; but finally her anger cooled, and she began to look objectively at what she had heard. For eighteen years she had

had nothing but admiration. Her father adored her, and her brothers had protected her and spoiled her. Now they were used to deferring to her judgment, since they discovered she had an uncanny way with the horses. The servants in the house and around the stables thought her perfect, although Mrs. Keever had tried to correct her boyish ways when she was younger. She had had a tutor for a short time instead of a governess, simply because the boys needed some education, but as she grew older, and the tutor showed signs of falling in love with her, he had been dismissed. The younger boys were going away to school now.

The young men of the neighborhood had all fallen under her spell, even the ones a head shorter, she recalled with a giggle. It was an accepted fact that Tom Gilroy was at the top of the lists to win her hand, and not only because his father's farm marched with that of the earl's. Kathleen Mary had not given it much thought; it was in the realm of "someday," and she had been happy and busy with the farm and her beloved horses. Now she had been brought face to face with the realization that there was more to life than horses, and the world was considerably bigger than Evelon Farm, and that everyone did not think her perfect.

Oh, she would love to show the arrogant duke that he was wrong! But how? This impossible question milled around in her brain for days, until she thought of her grandmother.

She had heard over the years that this proud lady was in the very height of the fashionable world. Surely she was her entree to that world, if only she could be persuaded to sponsor her granddaughter!

The letter proved impossible to write. One version was too humble and seemed to be begging for attention, for all the world like a poor relation with no home. The next was too arrogant—"I beg to inform your Lady"—and pride would not meet pride easily. When she tried a third time to explain why she wished to meet her grandmother, that seemed too forward. For revenge? On a man she had met briefly once?

For several days she pondered the situation until her father was secretly convinced that she had seen that her idea of a visit would never work, so he was totally unprepared for the radiant Katie who danced into the breakfast room one morning, full of tremendous plans.

"Father!" she exclaimed, kissing the top of his head. "It's solved! I have been trying and trying to write a letter to Grandmother, and none of them seemed the least bit satisfactory. But now I have the answer! Instead of writing, I will just arrive at her estate at Hertfordshire. Surely her curiosity will be such that she will not turn me away without even a glimpse of me, and then I can explain so much more easily why I am there, and what . . ."

"Whoa, whoa, my girl!" Lord Malloy broke in. "Now that is out of the question! Ride up to her gate like some tradesman and beg admission? And how would you travel, and with whom? It is not at all the thing for a young girl to be jauntering around the countryside without a chaperone in attendance. I fear I have neglected your education sorely if so you think!"

"No, no, Father! I woudn't be jauntering! Isn't Michael taking the two mares to Lord Elton next week? I have looked it up in the atlas, and it is only a few miles from grandmother's estate. Surely my own brother would be enough of a chaperone, and we'd have the grooms, and . . ."

"But to go uninvited! To just appear at the door like some tinker! She'll never see you, Katie, never!"

"I shall explain I am traveling through Hertfordshire and in passing through her neighborhood took the opportunity of stopping to meet her. If she refuses to see me, or if . . ." she faltered slightly, "if she does not wish me to stay, I shall come home with Michael, and that will be the end of it. Please, Da, please let me try! It means so much to me."

"Well," Lord Malloy said slowly, "I suppose there is no harm in trying. I do not approve of this, miss, but if 'tis the only way to bring you down to earth again, perhaps you had better go with Michael. You must be ready to travel on Tuesday week, though. My Lord Elton was very definite about getting those mares in good time."

Kathleen Mary threw her arms around her father.

"Oh, I will be ready, never fear! I must give all kinds of instructions to Mrs. Keever so my clothes will be ready, and then there's Diablo, someone must exercise him for me since I can't take him with me, and you mustn't forget, Father, that Silver has that sore hock that must be attended to . . ."

A thousand problems ran through her mind as she hastened away to begin planning her trip. She felt sure of success. What kind of grandmother would not even wish at least a peek at her daughter's only child? And once she had gained admission, she would know how to handle the situation, she was sure.

CHAPTER III

(A Confrontation with Lady Montgomery)

Several hectic days later, as she rode up the avenue to Greywood, she felt a distinct flutter of alarm that perhaps she had underestimated the problem. The drive was so long, so stately. She glanced down at her best riding habit. Why hadn't she noticed how shabby it was? She was riding sidesaddle in deference to convention, and she had tried hard that morning in the inn to do up her hair in what she thought might be a fashionable hairdo, but Michael had rushed her so, she eventually just brushed it well and tied it back with a ribbon. At least it wouldn't fall down over her ears when she removed her riding bonnet, as her first attempt had threatened to do! Her mouth tightened, and her chin went up. All she could do was try, and she had solved many other problems in her young life, after all. Michael, riding beside her, was struck dumb with awe. Even Lord Elton's estate had not been like this! Where was the house? They seemed to have been trotting up this avenue for miles! Around a curve in the drive they went, and both involuntarily pulled up their horses as the

manor came into view before them. It was still
a good distance away, and the woods opened
up to frame a charming vista of fields, then
gardens, and finally an ornamental lake which
reflected the towering home of Lady Montgomery. Even at this distance it seemed huge.

"Katie," Michael said tentatively, eyeing the
massive wings and turrets before him, "it's not
too late to turn back, you know."

At this timid remark, Kathleen Mary's chin
rose even higher. Setting the mare in motion,
she said,

"Turn back? When we have come so far?
Don't be a faintheart, Michael! She can't eat
us, after all!"

But when they had gained the front steps
stretching up and up to the massive front
doors, and when she perceived the stable boy
in livery who took charge of their horses, and
when their knock was answered by such an
impressive butler, she could not be sure. Her
voice was calm, however, as she gave her direction to the butler.

"Be so good as to inform Lady Montgomery
that her granddaughter Lady Kathleen Mary
Malloy and her brother Lord Michael Malloy
have called to see her."

The butler had seen many things in his long
life, but this was certainly the most surprising.
In spite of their unmodish clothes, both Michael and Kathleen Mary had what he called
"the look of quality." The fact that they were
grandchildren in a house where no one had

mentioned their names for twenty-five years
was, however, a test of his impassivity. He
inclined his head courteously.

"Certainly, m'lady. Perhaps you would care
to wait in this chamber while I ascertain if her
ladyship will receive you?"

So saying, he ushered them into a small
anteroom, and frowned at one of the footmen
who had so far forgotten himself as to stand
staring, his mouth open. He'll never go far,
Bright mused to himself, not for the first time,
as he offered refreshments to the travelers.

When they were settled in the beautiful
room, he proceeded up the winding staircase to
Lady Montgomery's boudoir, hoping his mistress had her salts handy when she heard his
news. He could have sent one of the footmen,
but he felt that this was a commission only he
could carry out. Behind him, he left two young
people, one squirming on the edge of a gold
satin chair of the French school, the other
gazing about her with interest while she tried
to still a suddenly racing heartbeat. It seemed
an age before the door opened again, but it was
only the footman, his face now schooled in
complete indifference that even Bright might
have applauded. He served them each a glass
of Madeira in beautiful long-stemmed crystal
goblets, and bowed himself out. Brother and
sister looked at each other as the door closed.

"It doesn't seem like you have the *entree,*
after all, Katie," Michael whispered, holding
his fragile glass carefully.

"It does appear to be taking forever, doesn't it? Perhaps she was resting." Kathleen Mary refused to be downcast at this point. The door opened, startling her. There stood the butler, a faint smile on his austere face. He inclined his head and, speaking directly to her, said,

"Her ladyship will receive you now, m'lady."

Brother and sister rose as one. A fleeting look of distress passed over Bright's impassive features.

"Lady Montgomery will receive her granddaughter alone." Bright moved to open the door and escort Kathleen Mary. She turned to Michael, confused by this turn of events, but he grinned at her suddenly and whispered,

"Go ahead, Katie, I'll wait right here for you. Didn't want to see the old lady anyway!" Raising his voice slightly, he added, "I'll be right here if you need me."

Kathleen Mary threw him a look of gratitude and prepared to follow Bright.

When Bright had first mounted the stairs and announced the visitors to Lady Montgomery, she had been resting, as was her wont at this time of day, so she had not been fully alert when he imparted his news. Of course she did not do anything as vulgar as "nap" in the middle of the day, but she had closed her eyes to rest them. This was perfectly understandable, since she had been perusing an extremely dull book of essays by the Reverend V——. The book slid to the floor with a distinct thud at the news Bright brought her. There was a moment of silence. The butler stood impassively waiting her orders. She sat up straighter and groped for her handkerchief.

"Have I heard you correctly, Bright?" she demanded haughtily.

"Yes, m'lady," Bright replied. "The young woman and her brother are even now partaking of some refreshment in the small salon."

"Well, I have no intention of seeing either one of them, and why you admitted them is beyond my comprehension. I am sure you are aware of my feelings on this subject."

The butler bowed his head. "Indeed, m'lady," he answered, and then looked the fierce old lady directly in the eye. "I have been happy in your service for many years, m'lady, and if I may be so bold . . ." He hesitated, and Lady Montgomery interrupted.

"Go on, man, go on! No need to pull your punches with me!"

"Just so, m'lady. I will admit to being startled when they appeared at the door. Such a look of her . . . of her mother the young woman has . . ." He paused, wondering if he had gone too far. Lady Montgomery stiffened but did not speak, so he continued. "The more I looked at her, ma'am, the more I thought that perhaps you would like to meet her, and her brother, of course."

"Never!" exclaimed the old lady. "I may consent, *may*, I remind you, to see this girl, but the brother can cool his heels below. He is undoubtably the image of his Irish father, and that I will not tolerate!"

She paused, too upset to continue. Bright interposed smoothly, "So I shall escort the young lady to you, m'lady?"

"No, wait, Bright! Oh, dear . . . yes, I suppose you had better. Why I continue to put up with your bullying I will never know!"

Lady Montgomery adjusted her flounces testily, while Bright smiled to himself, although no change of emotion showed on his face. Now it was his idea, but he knew that it was only to save face that Lady Montgomery had explained it that way. He turned and left the room.

Perhaps if the day had not been so gloomy, or the book of essays so dull, or perhaps if Lady Montgomery had been fully awake when Bright made his startling announcement, Kathleen Mary would never have gained admittance to her grandmother's presence. Even as Lady Montgomery waited, she wished she could call her butler back and have him turn them from her door. For many years she had mourned the loss of her beautiful, willful daughter. Such a future as she had had, with a duke on the point of proposing, and heaven knows how many other London beaus at her feet. And then to throw herself away on a practically penniless horse trader with only that useless Irish title and his good looks to commend him! It still caused a pain under her heart to remember. She had heard the gossip about her

daughter's marriage, even though she never
mentioned her name again—and all those children—one right after the other! It was somehow obscene, like rabbits, she thought with a
sniff. And then to die in childbirth with the
last one. She was aware that this girl was her
only granddaughter, that the rest were a pack
of boys, and nothing on this earth would in-
duce her to receive a one of them! If Bright
had not mentioned the likeness to Evelyn, she
might have stood her ground, but suddenly she
realized that she had been mourning her
daughter all the years of her marriage, long
before her untimely death. When that piece of
news came to her ears it had meant nothing.
For her, Evelyn had been dead from her wedding day. I must be getting senile, she thought,
otherwise I would never consent to this! The
door to the boudoir opened after a discreet
knock. Bright announced, in a voice from
which all color had fled,

"The Lady Kathleen Mary Malloy, ma'am."

He stepped to one side, and there on the
threshold stood a tall, tanned young woman
with chestnut hair, who looked directly at her
grandmother and seemed to be frozen in the
doorway.

"Good God!" that lady exclaimed. "Bright
didn't mention you were an Amazon! Well,
come in, come in! Don't just stand there like
a rabbit facing a stoat!! I won't eat you!"

Kathleen Mary advanced toward the chaise
where her grandmother was seated, gazing

around her in wonder. Never had she seen such
an apartment. It was crowded with all manner
of furniture and bric-a-brac, none of which
seemed to match, and all of it placed with a
complete disregard for the ankles and elbows of
unwary guests. A bright fire burned in the
fireplace on one wall, making the room extremely hot, and the heavy red-velvet drapes
were closed, which seemed to increase the tem-
perature. In one corner stood an elaborate bird
cage, the home of a drooping parrot who stared
at her disconsolately. But the most fantastic
feature of the room was surely her grandmother! She sat on the chaise, rigidly upright.
Her afternoon dress of purple mousseline was
adorned with heavy flounces of lace and knots
of gold ribbons. On her massive bosom rested
several brooches and a pince-nez which even
now she was raising to survey her guest. The
rings and bracelets she wore must surely have
worn down a frailer old lady! It was impossible
to distinguish the color of her hair, since she
wore it powdered, in the old style. Topping the
confection of curls and braids was a massive
head of nodding plumes. Kathleen Mary had
the sudden idea that that was why the parrot
looked so undone. Perhaps her grandmother
had just that morning decided to pluck some of
his tail feathers for her toilette! This thought
brightened her expression as she reached the
old lady, and curved her lips in a slight smile
which immediately brought into play the deep
dimple beside her mouth.

Good God! the old lady thought again. She may be almost six feet tall and have THAT MAN'S red hair, but she had Evelyn's face, right down to that dimple!

"Good afternoon, ma'am," Kathleen Mary said with as much dignity as she could muster while being stared at so intensely.

"Well, my girl, at least you do not have a vulgar Irish accent, which I had quite expected! Sit down opposite me. You are such a giantess that I will get a crick in my neck if I have to continue to look up at you from such a distance."

As Kathleen Mary took her seat across from the lady, she continued, "And to what do I owe the pleasure of this visit? I am sure you are aware that all converse between me and your family ceased many years ago. So why do you show up, uninvited, now?"

The old lady bristled at the thought. How she was put upon!

Kathleen Mary tried to compose her thoughts. Whatever she had expected she had not thought she would immediately have to jump into the middle of her story. She wished she had given more thought to how she would go about it; in the meantime, here was this angry old woman staring at her indignantly, and waiting for her explanation.

"I have a request to make of you, ma'am," she stammered.

"A request?" Lady Montgomery seemed to swell. "A request? To ask of me? La, one can hardly credit it! For twenty-five years there has been no intercourse between us, and now you appear, as bold as brass, and say you have a request to make. It hardly bears thinking of!"

She paused for breath and reached for her vinaigrette on a crowded table near the chaise. Clutching the bottle, along with her salts and her handkerchief, she continued.

"I must reply, young woman, that I had not thought to hear such boldness! The modern miss has surely lost all delicacy of feeling! I wonder at you, truly I do!"

Kathleen Mary was bewildered, but she put up her chin, again reminding her grandmother poignantly of her daughter.

"I am sorry, m'lady, if I have startled you," she began again. "I do not know who else to ask, and my father only consented to my seeing you after . . ."

"Your father!" Lady Montgomery interrupted with loathing. "We will have no mention of THAT MAN in this house, or I will order you to leave immediately."

Kathleen Mary rose with dignity, as angry now as her grandmother.

"In that case, m'lady, I will take my leave of you. Whatever you may feel about him, I must remind you he is my father, and I will not stand by and hear him slandered."

With a slight bow, she turned to the door, missing the look of chagrin on Lady Montgomery's face.

"Stop!" that lady commanded. "Come back

here and sit down. No one will slander your ... er ... your father. I wish to hear what you would ask of me, but perhaps you would be so kind as to launder your story of unseemly references to THAT MAN!"

It was a major concession, if Kathleen Mary had but realized it. She resumed her place, however, and waited for her grandmother to continue.

"Well, gel, what is this request? Do I have to pull it out of you like a bad tooth?"

"I see I had better be frank with you, ma'am. I have been very happy for all of my life until recently. At that time two gentlemen from London came to Evelon Farm to buy horses, and I heard them talking about me."

Her eyes flashed with indignation as she remembered, and her grandmother thought, Ah! What a beauty she is! The hearts she would break! However, she merely said, "Go on, girl, go on!"

"These two Corinthians discussed me when they did not think I could hear them. One of them was very complimentary, and I admit I was pleased to hear how taken with me he was. But the other one!" Her voice rang with loathing. "The other one! He did not agree with his friend that I was anything out of the common way. In fact he said I was 'perfect for my setting' and would be ridiculed in London by someone called the 'Beau.'"

"Yes, yes, Beau Brummel, he meant," the old lady interposed.

"Well, I did not know who he meant, but he was extremely insulting. How dare he say those things! I determined to prove him wrong, and when I cast about in my mind, it occurred to me that if you would sponsor me, I would be able to go to London, attend the smartest social evenings, and make a liar out of him once and for all! I do not care if he is the king himself, although he is only a duke, he had no right to speak in that slighting, superior way!"

Lady Montgomery interruped. "A duke, you say? What was his name?"

On learning that the abominable duke was none other than Giles Brentwood, her expression became thoughtful. After a pause, she said, "Yes, of course he upset you. Giles takes a great delight in being as upsetting as possible, which I think is the result of boredom. He has been fawned over for so long for his title and his money, he has lost any regard he might have had for other people's feelings. But take a look at yourself! In fact, stand up and turn around so I can see you better."

As Kathleen Mary obeyed, the old lady snorted.

"He was right, you know! Look at you, drab and undistinguished! Where had you that horrible habit? And your hair! It looks like one of your own horse's tails! And your face, good gad!"

Kathleen Mary turned back to her, looking puzzled.

"But I always thought my face was all right.

Everyone tells me how beautiful I am . . ."

"Oh, yes, my girl, you would have a beautiful face—if you hadn't burned it to a crisp! You look like some kind of red Indian! And your hands!"

Kathleen Mary looked at them in bewilderment.

"They are as tanned as your face, and your nails have obviously never been cared for. You look like you have been mucking out a stable for years!"

"They are quite clean, ma'am!" said Kathleen Mary indignantly.

"Naturally I am talking about their softness, since one assumes that even in Ireland a lady is taught to wash. And another thing, you are much too tall! The fashion now is for fragile blondes, not enormous redheads! I fear your noble gentleman was right. What have you learned all these years? Can you sing, or play the harp? How is your needlework? What dances have you learned? In short, what has been your education as a young lady of quality?"

Kathleen Mary drew herself up to her entire five feet nine inches.

"I have no graces, m'lady," she replied with dignity. "Is that so important to the fashionable world? I can do any job in the stable or on the farm with the best of men. I can ride any horse in the world, broken or not, and where I come from these qualities are more important than becoming a simpering miss, drooping over her embroidery and fainting at the least alarm!"

Lady Montgomery cackled suddenly.

"Gad, you have my spirit! I like that! But you can see that in an elegant ballroom you will not likely be required to break a horse!"

Kathleen Mary moved back to her chair and perched on the edge of it. Leaning toward her grandmother she asked,

"Are they so hard to learn, these accomplishments? I am not stupid, ma'am, and I would try very hard!"

Lady Montgomery looked at her with a shrewd eye.

"I believe you would, and you are right. They can be learned, and who better than I to teach you what you would have to know? You will have to unlearn a great deal, and it will cost a great deal of money . . ."

Kathleen Mary interrupted. "I have some money of my own, ma'am, from my mother."

"Tush! That little pittance from her aunt? It wouldn't buy half of what you need. But do not worry about that, child. Money is the least of our worries. I wish you were not so tall, that is the main problem."

"But Grandmother," said Kathleen Mary, calling her thus for the first time, "surely you can set fashion! Perhaps next season little blondes will be quite outside the pale!"

Lady Montgomery chuckled as there was a discreet knock on the door. Bright appeared bearing a tray of refreshments and looking slightly apprehensive. He had been relieved when the visit had not terminated quickly, but he had wondered what the two ladies had been saying all this time. As he stood before them, Lady Montgomery said,

"Well, Bright, and what are you staring at? Fetch the housekeeper to me at once. My granddaughter is making an indefinite stay with me. I want the blue bedchamber prepared, and you had better apprise the agent that I will want to speak to him first thing in the morning."

She turned to Kathleen Mary.

"Well, gel, there is no turning back. You're sure this is what you want? From now on you must obey *my* orders explicitly, for it will not be easy to turn from a country miss to a lady in high society in a few months. My first order is this—from now on you will be known as the Lady Kathleen; Kathleen Mary is too, too terribly Irish!"

Kathleen swallowed hard, but her eyes were sparkling.

"Yes, I am sure . . . very sure!"

"Very well. Tell Bright where your trunks are, and he will arrange to have them delivered to Greywood. Now you had better say goodbye to the young man belowstairs. I am sure he is about ready to storm the ramparts and rescue you from the wicked witch!"

"Michael! I had forgotten him!" Kathleen exclaimed. "Excuse me, ma'am!" In a whirl of skirts, she flew out the door.

Bright and Lady Montgomery looked at each other. The eyes of both were suspiciously damp. Finally she spoke.

"I hope you are happy now, Bright. See what your bullying has brought us to! Heaven will have to help us turn that girl into anything remotely resembling a debutante, for I do not know why I have consented to such a wild scheme. I must be bewitched!"

As Bright turned to go, his only words were a respectful, "Just so, m'lady!"

CHAPTER IV

(Lady Kathleen Becomes a Lady)

In the days and weeks that followed, Kathleen worked harder than she had ever imagined possible. The hardest thing to get used to at first was her confinement to the house. Greywood was more than spacious, comprising some fifty bedchambers and rooms for attendants, several drawing rooms, even a grand ballroom, but Kathleen was so used to spending most of her time at the stables or out riding that she felt stifled. The mare she had ridden from Ireland languished in her stall, and had to be exercised by a groom. One afternoon, while sitting with her grandmother in one of the smaller salons, she could not refrain from a sigh. The afternoon was bright, with just a slight breeze—a perfect day for a ride! Lady Montgomery eyed her sharply.

"And what was that sigh for, miss? Have you made another error in that needlework?"

"I'm sorry, Grandmother," Kathleen said. "I was thinking of this lovely afternoon and wishing I might go riding. You know, I was used to ride every day, no matter what the weather." She looked pleadingly at her grandmother.

"Well, I see no reason why you cannot have a ride. Yes, it would be good for you to get some exercise. I had forgotten that part of the program, since it is the one area that does not require tutoring."

Then, as Kathleen jumped up in happiness, she exclaimed,

"Sit down at once, young lady! How dare you leap from your chair in that vulgar manner? Now (as Kathleen sat once again), rise and take your leave of me as you have been taught."

Demurely, Kathleen gathered her skirts and stood up, back straight, head up. She turned to Lady Montgomery and curtsied.

"Oh, dear, I wobbled again!" she cried.

"A distinct wobble, I'm afraid. Curtsy ten times more, and then you may go."

As Kathleen complied, a small frown of concentration on her face, Lady Montgomery continued,

"Smile, girl! We are having enough problems with your complexion without adding wrinkles! I do not think that cucumber lotion is working. Perhaps tonight we will try the strawberry cream to fade that tan. Mind you, wear a large-brimmed hat, and gloves. I am sorry your new habits are not yet delivered from town, but I do not expect anyone to see you. Be sure you stay on the estate grounds. The groom will tell you where you should ride. And Kathleen"—as she prepared to leave—"a ladylike ride, if you please!"

A retort rose to her lips, but Kathleen swallowed it and agreed.

And so, every fine afternoon that followed, Kathleen and a groom rode about the estate. It was not long before she had the entire staff of the stables eating out of her hand, and the "ladylike rides" lasted only until she was out of sight, in case her grandmother should be looking. Fitton, the head groom, even went so far as to ask her opinion of a new type of poultice he was using on a sore hock, a sure sign of approbation, since he had the reputation of being an old curmudgeon, and very strict. Kathleen treated him as she had Matthews, and they got on together famously.

Still, she could not spend anywhere near as much time as she wished in the stables or on horseback. Every day was parceled out to various lessons. A drawing teacher had been engaged and just as abruptly dismissed when it was found that no amount of instruction would suffice to teach Kathleen perspective and line. Lady Montgomery sighed and crossed sketching parties from her list of Kathleen's future engagements.

She went to great trouble to import a dancing master from London. He had to be tall enough so Kathleen did not tower over him. Her grandmother turned down several applications for the post and was beginning to feel that gentlemen over five and a half feet did not enter the profession, when Mr. Deerfield was found. This young man was enchanted with his lovely pupil, but since all lessons were conducted under the watchful eye of Lady Montgomery, nothing came of it but some sleepless nights, while Kathleen learned the various country dances, gavottes, and the new rage, the waltz. She was rather better at dancing than art.

Needlework had to be accounted a failure, however. None of her embroidery or lacework was fit for anything but dustcloths, as Lady Montgomery tartly pointed out. Since there was not enough time to learn the pianoforte or harp—a circumstance for which Kathleen was most sincerely thankful— she was given vocal instruction. She had a sweet, true tone, though somewhat low, and appeared at her best when singing the simpler folk songs, but that of course was not at all the thing, so she was forced to learn an aria and some German lieder for tone. She did not mention to her grandmother how much she loathed them all.

By this time it was instinctive for her never to slouch, and to move gracefully. Lady Montgomery had been blunt about the importance of this.

"Understand, my girl, since you are tall, you must hold yourself up, and not appear to be trying to accommodate a smaller gentleman. If you slouch, you merely call attention to your inches. You must be proud of them, to carry them off. And, of course, a Montgomery never slouches."

Some new clothes had arrived from London,

and as Lady Montgomery had anticipated,
made it much easier to discipline Kathleen's
mannish stride. The new styles with their narrow skirts falling straight from a high Empire
waist made a dainty step a necessity. The first
time Kathleen had tried to walk in a new
creation of deep yellow muslin trimmed with
enchanting ribbons streaming from a knot
called "Cupid's Passion," she had split the
gown from hem to knee, and it had to be
dispatched back to town for repairs. After that
she was more careful. Her grandmother had
overseen all her new clothes, and Kathleen was
feminine enough to approve of the confections
that appeared almost daily from the better
modistes, although she wondered what it was
costing, there seemed to be so many of them.
Walking dresses, habits, morning gowns, gowns
for balls, for teas, for the country—all with
their accompanying slippers and bonnets,
shawls and reticules, to say nothing of the
various underthings, stockings, gloves, and
nightwear.

There was one item of clothing that Lady
Montgomery knew nothing about, however.
Kathleen's new personal maid adored her mistress, and she was an excellent seamstress.
With many giggles and whispered conferences,
she made Kathleen a riding skirt to her specifi-
cations. It was a split skirt so she could ride
astride, but so cleverly was it fashioned that it
appeared to be merely a regular riding skirt
when she was standing. Kathleen had it made

in black velvet, with a very severely cut jacket
to match. She planned to wear it with shiny
black boots, a man's riding cap, and no color
other than a white blouse. In fact, if her plans
worked out, and she could get her grandmother
to let her send for Diablo, the only color would
be white lace at her throat and wrists, and her
own chestnut hair, now coiffed and curled in
a fashionable fringe.

How she missed Evelon Farm and Diablo!
She was often homesick for her father, the
boys, and the horses she loved, but no matter
how often she felt sad, she could always regain
her composure by remembering Giles
Brentwood and his arrogant dismissal of her.

Even at the table she was not free of lessons.
First she had to learn the bewildering array of
plate and crystal; which fork was used with
each dish; how to refuse the wine; and how to
eat so daintily that it appeared she was not
eating at all. This was very hard, since she was
always hungry. Lady Montgomery had decreed
a weight loss of ten pounds at least. Kathleen
might not be a fragile blonde, but with the loss
of a few pounds, she could be considered
willowy.

As if this weren't enough, she had to carry
on imaginary conversations with those seated
to her left and right. Lady Montgomery decided who the guests would be each evening;
one night a bishop, the next a high-nosed
patroness of Almack's, sometimes a persistent
suitor that Kathleen had to learn to dis-

courage. The butler and footmen soon grew accustomed to the two ladies seated at the long dining room table, one correcting and instructing, the other turning to the vacant seat beside her and exclaiming,

"La, sir, your knowledge of politics is overwhelming! Pray tell me what you think of the prime minister's latest start?"

Lady Montgomery had no fear she would turn Kathleen into a simpering miss, her sense of humor and quick wit were too good. One evening in the drawing room, awaiting the tea she would have to pour out to her grandmother's satisfaction, she began to converse with an imaginary gentleman she called "Lord Fudd." In no time at all, tears of laughter were streaming down her grandmother's face.

"I protest, Lord Fudd!" she exclaimed, drawing back from this impetuous mystery guest. "I fear I have never thought of you in this manner. Release my hand! You must know that matrimony is not one of my aims. Please to rise! The other guests are staring at you. I do not think it at all the thing to propose in a crowded drawing room, even if I have enchanted you with my rendering of your favorite aria!"

Bright, bringing in the tea tray, was delighted to hear his mistress laughing. It had been many long years since he had heard any such merriment in this house. From that time on, he became Kathleen's champion, and gave

her many a hint on protocol and behavior as
seen from the servants' hall.

In fact, the whole establishment was interested in Kathleen's success, with the exception of her ladyship's maid, Griffin. This austere personage was not pleased with the
amount of activity she was forced to expend
now that that "Irish hoyden" had joined the
household. Griffin was shrewd enough to hide
this from Lady Montgomery, although she
dropped many stories about Kathleen, generally connected with her failures, and com-
miserated with her mistress on the impossibili-
ty of her task. She had spoken sharply to
Kathleen just once, when she was alone with
her, but she would never repeat it. Kathleen
had drawn herself up even straighter and said
quietly and coldly, "You may retire, Griffin. If
I have any further trouble with you, I shall be
forced to report it to my grandmother." The
maid left in confusion. A duchess could not
have handled it better, but then, Kathleen.
although free and easy with the servants, in-
stinctively knew her place and consequence
and never stepped over the bounds of propriety.

At last Lady Montgomery declared herself
satisfied. She decided it was time to put Kathleen to the test, and better to do it at
Greywood than in London. The season was fast
approaching, and they would have to begin
planning to move the household to her large
town house in Eaton Square, but before that

there would be a small evening party at Greywood, with some of the country personages that Lady Montgomery considered worthy of her attention.

And so, one fine evening in early January, the carriages streamed up the drive to the doors of Greywood while Kathleen stood beside her grandmother at the head of the massive stairs. Her toilette had taken much time, and Lady Montgomery was very pleased with her appearance when she made her entrance to her ladyship's room. She wore a gown of muslin, deceptively simple, but obviously made for her by one of London's leading *modistes*. No pink or pale blue for Kathleen! The gown was a deep shade of blue, matching her eyes exactly. She wore no ornaments but her mother's pearl necklet, and a small pearl brooch at her corsage that Lady Montgomery had given her for her come-out.

"At least your *first* come-out, for this one does not really count, Kathleen," she informed her. "Yes, you will do very well, you are in looks this evening, and your skin is finally as white as can be wished for. Now we will see if you can carry off the rest."

So Kathleen curtsied as she greeted the guests, and smiled and chatted with the gentlemen who were enchanted with this new paragon, and was pleasant and attentive to the old ladies, and easy with the other young ladies, several of whom were not at all pleased to meet her. And who could blame them? All

but the most attentive of their suitors deserted
them for the tall, beautiful redhead. Lady
Montgomery's heart swelled with pride. The
girl did just as she ought. She was a success.
Well, blood would tell!

She might not have been so pleased if she
had seen the wink Kathleen gave Bright as he
passed through the dining room bearing a tray
of champagne. A young gentleman, all of five
feet four inches, was even then trying to fix her
attention, unaware that he looked more than
slightly ridiculous beside her. Bright of course
did not respond in any way, although perhaps
a muscle twitched for a fleeting moment in his
face.

The next morning, sharing chocolate with
her grandmother, Kathleen learned that she
was now ready to take London by storm. Plans
would be set in motion for the fourgon to
remove such items of the household as Lady
Montgomery deemed indispensable to her comfort, along with the many trunks and boxes.
Then would follow the coach with Bright and
the other servants. Only when all was in order,
would Kathleen and her grandmother and their
personal maids ride to London in easy stages in
that lady's magnificent town coach.

There were some months before the season
would properly begin, but Lady Montgomery
felt she had been inured in the country long
enough. She had had to forgo a Christmas
house party with dear friends and several other
interesting events that winter because of Kath-

leen's training—not that she really minded, for
she was becoming quite attached to her granddaughter, and hadn't felt so well in years.
Their early arrival in town would insure Kathleen's feeling of ease there once the season did
begin. Lady Montgomery was so pleased and so
full of plans that Kathleen felt she could in-
troduce the scheme that had been long on her
mind.

"Grandmother," she began, as Lady Montgomery paused for breath, "may I please send to
Ireland for my horse? I have missed Diablo so
much, and I know he must be pining for me
too. You know how you have said I appear to
best advantage on horseback, and there will
surely be opportunities to ride in the park and
on excursions."

Her grandmother was puzzled. "Why, what is
wrong with the mare you have here? A very
pretty piece of horseflesh, so Flitton tells me,
and being a chestnut is stunning with your
hair." Then seeing the disappointment in
Kathleen's face, she added, "Oh, very well. You
may send for this other mare, Diablo, did you
call her?"

Before she thought, Kathleen said, "Oh,
Diablo is a stallion, Grandmother. Wait 'til you
see him! He is coal black and so beautiful! I
know my father will send him, since he is not
needed at stud right now, although . . ."

Lady Montgomery's expression was so horrified that Kathleen's explanation died away.

"A *stallion*? No lady rides a stallion! A

gentle mare, that is quite unexceptionable, but a stallion is out of the question!"

Kathleen saw that further pleading would be in vain and would distress her grandmother. She managed to swallow her disappointment, for her grandmother had done so much for her she did not feel she could beg for further indulgences. She resolutely put from her mind the vision of herself riding her black stallion dressed all in black herself, and passing the Duke of Havenhall as if he were standing still. This dream had different endings. On some occasions she never allowed him to catch her, gallop as he would. At other times she slid from Diablo's back into his eager arms. And then . . . and then? She shook her head, not understanding her thoughts at all.

Lady Montgomery also thought of Giles occasionally. Since she had heard Kathleen mention his name as the arrogant duke in their first interview, she had been amused to daydream of Kathleen's catching him; son of the very same duke she had planned for her daughter Evelyn to marry! It would make it all worthwhile, finally.

CHAPTER V

(Lady Kathleen Discovers Polite Society)

When Lady Montgomery and Kathleen finally took coach for London, it was a crisp, clear day in early February. The journey seemed interminable to Kathleen. There were several stops to visit friends and relatives, leisurely nuncheons, refreshments at each posting house where they changed horses, and long evenings in private parlors of the best inns, which Lady Montgomery graced with her patronage. Kathleen enjoyed the attention they were given, from the obsequiousness of mine host, to the bustle of the servants as they hastened to serve them. Surely her grandmother must be a very important person to command such obeisance.

At last they rode into the London streets at dusk, and Kathleen's eyes were wide with excitement and interest. So busy it was, with people and horses, carriages and drays, elegant sedan chairs, and vendors crying their wares! After the quiet of the country, the noise was deafening; never at Evelon or later at Greywood could Kathleen have imagined such a din—she wondered if she would be able to sleep at all! Their way took them through the overcrowded, poorer sections, and Kathleen saw thin children barely covered even in the chill winter evening, and smelled the overpowering stench from the open drains and rotting vegetation. As they approached Eaton Square, however, all signs of poverty disappeared, and the elegant homes with their pillars and grand doorways each seemed more beautiful than the last.

Bright was on hand as the coach drew up to a massive house, its portico brightly lit by flares, and two footmen in Montgomery livery hurried out to assist the ladies and their maids to alight.

"Welcome, m'lady, Lady Kathleen," the old butler beamed. "I trust you have had a pleasant journey?"

Lady Mongomery snorted. "Pleasant? I would hardly call it that! I feel as if each trip to London takes longer and is more uncomfortable than the last. The state of the roads is a disgrace! One surely would expect Parliament to attend to them, unless it is a new war strategy to slow Napoleon if he decides to invade! We will go directly to our rooms, Bright, and tell the chef that only a simple dinner will be required."

Lady Montgomery mounted the steps, closely followed by Kathleen, while delivering this tirade. As they entered the hall, she was surprised to see what must surely be the entire staff of servants. Her grandmother moved to greet them individually and to carefully note the names of any new members of the household. She then introduced her granddaughter, and Kathleen, although standing easily erect as she had been taught, was slightly appalled at the pairs of eyes fastened on her.

At last it was done, and the two ladies were free to retire to their rooms. Clara, Kathleen's maid, was ecstatic with the arrangements, and Kathleen too admired the large bedchamber that was to be hers. It was done in soft shades of green with striped upholstery—"all the latest crack, m'lady!" as Clara informed her. A comfortable dressing room with large closets completed the accommodations. Kathleen sank down thankfully in a large wing chair before the bright fire blazing on the hearth, while Clara began to unpack.

That night, after the "simple" dinner—only three courses and four removes—when she retired, she lay in the comfortable bed and dreamily watched the fire. At last she was here! At last she could show the Duke of Havenhall that he was wrong! She could hardly wait to begin.

The following days were taken up with shopping and afternoon calls. Kathleen had never imagined such shops, filled with such enticing goods and beautiful displays. Although she had thought she had enough clothes to last her indefinitely, it seemed that was not the case. She was fitted with several new gowns and accessories, for, as her grandmother pointed out, it would be fatal to be seen wearing the same outfit too many times.

Kathleen would have loved to explore London, but when she proposed this to her horrified grandmother, she received quite a lecture.

"Go to museums? Look at monuments? 'Fore gad, do you want to be known as a bluestocking? You will do just as I say, miss, and if London is too thin of company just yet for balls and soirees, at least it will give you an opportunity to meet some people who will be useful to know later in the season."

And so Kathleen accompanied her grandmother to what she privately termed "old lady tea parties," and was as demure and polite as she knew how to be. She also met some other young ladies, but with a few exceptions, this could not be said to be a success. Kathleen called them "missish," and in truth there was little she could find to say to them. They appeared to be taken up with clothes, hairstyles, and who was going to catch whom this season. When she mentioned this to her grandmother, the old lady was stunned.

"But of course they are concerned about marriage!" she exclaimed. "Have you not yet realized that this is the Marriage Mart? Why else would parents bring their daughters to town, expend heaven knows how much money on their clothes and on balls unless they expected them to marry, and to marry well, as soon as possible?"

Kathleen spoke slowly. "No, I didn't realize it, Grandmother. I had no thought of marriage in my mind, only . . ." She stopped, confused about how to explain her real motive for visiting London. Suddenly her chin went up, in that now familiar gesture. *She* had no intention of seeking a husband, no matter what society thought! Lady Montgomery watched her sharply.

"You were about to say, gel?"

Kathleen's eyes twinkled. "Why, only, Grandmother, that the whole thing reminds me forcibly of a horse fair! Up on the block, paraded before all so your good points can be admired, and any faults hidden as carefully as might be. They even dye horses to get a matched pair, the unscrupulous dealers, and only yesterday Miss Booth told me that nature had not blessed her with blond enough curls, but she had found a marvelous hairdressing shop that promised to do wonders!"

The old lady cackled while trying to look shocked.

"'Pon rep, Kathleen! What a thing to say! Girls and horses! Of course there are parents who do appear to be searching for the highest bidder; that I must admit in all honesty."

Kathleen interrupted quickly. "*You* have no such intention, do you, ma'am? I must tell you that I do not wish to marry!"

Her grandmother bit back the retort that she had been about to utter. No sense getting the gel riled, and time would take care of her scruples about marriage. Well she knew she had made a mistake with her daughter, trying to force her into a loveless marriage. With Kathleen she intended to be more careful, just as she intended to eliminate undesirable beaus by whatever means at her command, if Kathleen should show a *tendre* for any of them. She was quite aware why Kathleen had been so intent on coming to town, but she was playing a very close hand. Let her think marriage was expected, and she would bolt for the home stable. So she smoothed her skirts and said casually,

"Of course you shall do just as you please. I have no authority over you, after all, it is entirely up to THAT MAN. But I caution you, Kathleen, to watch your style of conversation. If you mention horse trading in connection with marriage, you will not have to worry about proposals, for you will become a positive antidote!"

Kathleen laughed and gave Lady Montgomery a hug and a kiss which upset her cap but nonetheless pleased her very much.

Since London seemed to be devoid of men except for a few callow grandsons who appeared at the tea parties as briefly as they dared, Kathleen began to wonder why the season was named the Marriage Mart at all, for it was surely a misnomer, but eventually the great trickled back to town from their country homes and retreats.

It was generally agreed that the Axminster ball opened the London season that year. The duchess was presenting her oldest daughter to society, and no expense was spared to make the occasion memorable. Kathleen and Lady Montgomery were among the guests, and when Kathleen saw the style of the duke's London establishment, and the numbers of distinguished guests, she did not wonder any more about her grandmother's insistence that she look her best that evening. As she had been dressing, Lady Montgomery appeared to supervise the proceedings, a circumstance that threw Clara into some alarm. Kathleen was surprised, since what seemed like endless discussions had already taken place about her dress, the style of her hair, and her jewels. Kathleen could not help feeling impatient at the time it was taking for her turnout. Lady Montgomery quickly apprised her of the situation in a few well chosen words while Clara was fetching Griffin to assist in the proceedings.

"You will be patient, my girl, and try to realize how very important your appearance is tonight. The cream of society will be there, and it will be the first time many of them will see you. I expect your behavior to be everything that is correct, and I cannot stress strongly enough that your appearance and conversation is of the first importance. Perhaps the Beau will be there, although it is early in the season, and if he ignores you, or even offers an unfavorable comment to a friend, you will be undone!"

Kathleen raised an eyebrow. "Surely, ma'am, I do not care what the gentleman thinks of me, or any other gentleman," she added darkly. "I know the Beau is the arbiter of fashion, but I refuse to kowtow to such arrogance! He can take me or leave me, I care not!''

Lady Montgomery spoke more sharply. "He will probably not even be aware you are alive! However, if he should ask to be presented, curb your dislike, if you please! He sets fashion, and if he decides that you are not to be in fashion, there is nothing you can do to change the situation. Do you understand me, miss? Tonight is the culmination of all our work, so tread softly!''

At this juncture Clara returned with Griffin, and Kathleen was bade to turn slowly while her grandmother and the two dressers studied her appearance. She was dressed in a deceptively simple gown of emerald green, a color that her grandmother had agonized over for many an hour. It was really too strong a shade for a debutante, but it set off Kathleen's fiery hair to perfection and insured that, whatever else, she would not disappear in the background of pinks, pale blues, and whites so favored by other young ladies and their mamas. Because Lady Montgomery had finally decided on the emerald gown, her accessories were almost severe. No dangling jewels, no wealth of flowers, no elaborate hairdo. Instead, she wore only a single emerald on a slender gold chain. Against her now faultless white throat it was superb. Her hair was dressed in a smooth style with only a few curls clustered at the back. As she slowly turned in the light, Lady Montgomery's eyes grew misty. She was lovely, no, more than that, exceptionally beautiful in spite of her height. Lady Montgomery worried most about that. There was no denying she would tower over many a gentleman, even in her flat silk slippers. She would not, however, tower over Giles Brentwood! At that pleasing thought, Lady Montgomery rose and announced she was satisfied. The two ladies descended the stairs, followed by their maids bearing their wraps and reticules. Bright ushered them to the carriage, which was waiting at the door, a special smile for Lady Kathleen.

"Ah, she is just as she should be, a beauty!" he thought. He knew from the look on Lady Montgomery's stern face how proud she was of her granddaughter, and with what *élan* she would present her to her friends. It would make up for all the chagrin she had felt all these years of her daughter's disappointing marriage.

When the carriage finally drew up to the portico after long delays because of the crowds, Kathleen gasped at the wealth and elegance displayed. She and her grandmother were ushered up a wide stairway after footmen and maids had taken their wraps, and then announced to the duke and duchess and their daughter by a portly *major domo* The duke was obviously taken with this beautiful young woman, but the duchess' eyes narrowed slightly, even as she smiled her welcome. It was no wonder, for her daughter Jane, sadly plump and plain, merely appeared fussy in her elaborate dress and fantastic jewels beside Kathleen's simple, tall elegance.

The duke's son pressed her hand fervently.

"M'lady! Where have you been hiding this

vision?" he breathed. "Surely I have not seen the Lady Kathleen before!"

Kathleen gently loosed her hand, although she remembered to smile and hide her dislike of this eager young man with his damp handclasp and almost lustful expression. Lady Montgomery drew Kathleen closer to her.

"My granddaughter is staying with me for the season," she replied. "She has just lately come from Ireland. She is my daughter Evelyn's child, and I have been delighted to welcome her." Thus, in one sentence, Lady Montgomery broke the silence of twenty-five years and established Kathleen's place in her affection, a fact the duke noted with a smile.

The two ladies than proceeded to the ballroom, but not until Frederick, the duke's son, had insisted on a dance. Kathleen shuddered inwardly but agreed with every sign of complaisance. As they walked away, she leaned down toward her grandmother and uttered one syllable —"ugh!" Lady Montgomery's face lifted into a smile, although she tapped Kathleen's knuckles with her fan.

"Just so, my dear, but you will dance with the young man regardless. How unfortunate dear Emily has been in her children, to be sure!"

The ballroom was decorated in delicate shades of yellow and festooned with flowers and candles. The enormous chandelier glistened with thousands of prisms and lit the fantastic scene below brilliantly. Kathleen stood spellbound on the threshold. Never had she imagined the grandeur of such a ball with the numerous guests, each more richly attired than the next. Her grandmother led her to a group near the door. The introductions were numerous, in fact, Kathleen soon realized that she could not remember half the people she was presented to. One face, however, she did recognize. Robert Marlow stood before her, admiration in his eyes. She was a bit piqued that he did not appear to know her until her name was announced. Then his face lit up.

"But surely I have met the Lady Kathleen before!" he exclaimed. "You are the same lady I met in Ireland at Evelon Farm, are you not?"

Kathleen demurely agreed that she was. Robert appeared to be dumbfounded.

"Well, my good man," her grandmother interrupted, "and are you so astounded by the coincidence? My granddaughter is making a stay with me during the season."

"Delightful, delightful!" he stammered. "It is only that I had not thought to see the lady here. I beg the honor of a dance!"

Kathleen consulted her card, which was fast being filled, and a country dance was agreed to, later in the evening. As Robert withdrew, her grandmother chuckled,

"Young idiot! He is certainly taken with you, my dear, to the point where he does not realize he would be at more of an advantage seated beside you where you would at least appear to be equal. In the dance you will have at least half a head on him and he will have to stare up at you, instead of at you!"

Kathleen agreed. "I hope, ma'am, that there are some tall men in society!" Her eyes had investigated the ballroom thoroughly, and there was no sign of Giles Brentwood.

The music began, and as soon as he had dispatched his duty dance with his sister, Lord Axminster appeared hastily before her. Kathleen rose dutifully and surrendered her hand, albeit reluctantly, to his damp clasp. She was glad she wore long kid gloves, for there was certainly more to this life than she had realized!

Her grandmother retired to the sidelines and several of her cronies, where she spent a remarkably enjoyable evening watching her granddaughter being sought after by many beaus, and informing her friends of just as many of the circumstances as she wished to divulge. She had also noted the absence of Giles Brentwood, but she was more pleased with it than Kathleen. Let Kathleen be established first, and talked about as one of the new beauties, and then we would see! Beau Brummel made an appearance after supper but was not presented to Kathleen and left shortly thereafter. Lady Montgomery wished he had noticed the sylph in the emerald gown, but there was plenty of time.

When they were finally seated in their carriage at the end of the ball, she enjoyed Kathleen's pungent comments about several of the people she had met, and greeted Bright with a beaming smile.

"An enjoyable evening, m'lady, I hope?" said the butler as he helped them with their wraps.

"Most enjoyable, Bright," the lady replied. "I cannot remember when I have had such a pleasant evening!"

Bright rightly interpreted this to mean that Lady Kathleen had been a success, and Lady Montgomery had enjoyed scoring off many an old acquaintance with her beautiful new granddaughter. It was obvious that many wounds had been repaid this evening!

He announced this to the housekeeper the next morning, and it was soon common knowledge among the staff that their young lady was soon to be one of the season's brightest stars.

"And," he added knowingly, "I do not think that the title 'Incomparable' is outside her grasp!"

From the times he opened the door that morning to accept the cards and invitations and several bouquets from admirers, it seemed he was right.

Kathleen in the meantime slept deeply and worried not at all about her success. Her only disappointment was that the Duke of Havenhall had not witnessed her triumph.

CHAPTER VI

(The Beau Approves—Enter Lord Ramsdale)

In the days that followed, Kathleen found herself in a whirl of balls, routs, Venetian breakfasts, riding parties, theater engagements, teas, and the inevitable shopping excursions. One delightful evening was spent at Ranelagh with a party of young people which included Robert Marlow, who had firmly attached himself to Kathleen. His friends might scoff at his devotion to a girl who literally looked down on him, but he was too smitten to consider any disadvantages. His good-natured face beamed happily whenever he saw her, and he always hastened to her side, making, as Lady Montgomery put it, "a perfect cake of himself." She was not worried that her granddaughter would lose her heart to any such as Robert Marlow, for Kathleen considered him merely a good friend, and treated him like one of her brothers, a fact that would have shattered Robert, had he but realized it. Kathleen's only disappointment with the London season so far was the fact that the duke had not yet appeared. In discreetly questioning his cousin she discovered that Giles was detained at his estates on a matter of business but was looked for any day. With this she had to be content.

One activity she would not forgo, no matter how late the party or strenuous the day, was her daily ride in the park. She expected her grandmother to disapprove, but Lady Montgomery was shrewdly aware that she showed most to advantage on the back of her chestnut mare. She was much too tall in the ballroom, there was no denying that, and only her extraordinary beauty saved her from joining the debutantes who had to have partners found for them. That beauty, combined with a ready wit and her inability to take herself seriously, won her many admirers, but the final seal of approval came from Beau Brummel himself. The Beau, riding sedately in the Axminster carriage with a party of friends, espied Kathleen in the park one afternoon. She was cantering along with only her groom in attendance, and because she was always happiest on horseback, her smiling face and glowing eyes caught his attention.

"A new face on our London scene," he remarked to the duchess. "Who is she, do you know?"

The duchess, sadly disappointed in her daughter Jane's season—for some reason, the girl just did not take—was slightly miffed. She had had to listen to her son's raptures about the lady on more than one occasion.

"That, my dear Beau," she replied tartly, "is

Lady Kathleen Malloy, and she is as Irish as her name!"

"But who are her relations?" The Beau pursued the subject firmly, to the duchess' chagrin.

"She is Lady Montgomery's granddaughter," Lord Elgin interrupted. "Surely you remember the tale of Lady Evelyn Montgomery who eloped at Gretna with an Irish earl! Her mother, who has never mentioned her name in twenty-five years, suddenly presents the granddaughter to society. The *on dit* of the year, my dear fellow, I do assure you!"

The duchess smirked. "One can only assume the Irish air grows Amazons! She is almost six feet tall, poor girl!"

The Beau smiled faintly, but all he replied was, "Unfortunate, but she is a superb rider and she has a beautiful face."

The rout given by Lady Gordan would live in Lady Montgomery's memory as the evening that Beau Brummel asked to be presented to Kathleen. Swelling with pride, she beckoned across the room to her granddaughter, who was laughing at a sally from the young gentleman who had just fetched her a glass of negus. As Kathleen approached, she recognized the impeccable gentleman awaiting her, and her eyes sparkled. The moment was at hand!

After the introduction, the Beau led her to a chair.

"I'm sure that you will be more comfortable

here, m'lady," he said. "These evenings can be so fatiguing, don't you agree?"

Kathleen forgot herself. "Thank you, sir," she smiled up at him as she seated herself. "And why do not these other gentlemen realize, as you do, that any time they can get me to sit down is a point to their advantage?"

The Beau seated himself beside her, one eyebrow raised.

"Oh, dear, will I never learn!" she exclaimed. "I promised Grandmother that I would be all complaisance, and the first thing I say is wrong!"

The Beau smiled. "Be yourself, my dear, I do advise you. London is strewn with insipid maidens who hardly dare lift their eyes or utter anything beyond a weak 'yes, m'lord.' If I remarked the sky was falling, they would only say, 'yes, m'lord, if you say so, m'lord.'"

Kathleen leaned toward him eagerly. "I am so glad to have your approval, sir! I find it quite the most difficult thing in society to be always saying just the opposite of what you are thinking! It is such a good thing that people can't see inside our heads, is it not?"

The Beau agreed, remembering some of his own thoughts this evening. Kathleen continued.

"I wonder if *doing* what you want is the same as *saying* what you think? What would you think if I rode a stallion in the park? I have the most beautiful stallion in Ireland and

I miss him very much, but my grandmother will not hear of my sending for him."

"So, you want me to set the seal of approval on this enterprise, do you? Leaving your grandmother with nothing to say? By all means ride your stallion! You ride superbly and show all our other ladies the way."

They continued chatting about horses and riding for several minutes. When the Beau learned that Diablo was coal black, his eyes narrowed slightly, and he appeared lost in thought. Presently he remarked,

"Ah, yes! May I suggest a black habit? That would surely make an unforgettable sight, with only your hair for color."

Kathleen blushed faintly, remembering the innovative riding skirt she had prepared, but she did not mention it. When a gentleman came to claim her for the dance whose sets were forming, she rose regretfully. She had enjoyed talking to the Beau, he was nothing at all like she had imagined. He smiled kindly at her.

"Remember what I told you, Lady Kathleen," he said, "and refer your grandmother to me if there is any opposition in that quarter."

Kathleen let her eyelids droop, hung her head shyly, and sighed languidly. "Yes, m'lord," she said demurely. "If you say so, m'lord."

The Beau laughed out loud and kissed her hand in parting, a fact not missed by Lady Montgomery and several indignant mamas.

The duchess of Axminster was incensed. If only he would do that for Jane, it would make all the difference! She did not realize that the Beau had already decided that Jane was of the company of insipid maidens and that he had no intention of distinguishing her in any way. Beau Brummel could not stand a bore, of either sex.

On that same evening, Kathleen also met Lord Ramsdale, a gentleman not as appreciated by Lady Montgomery as the Beau. Kathleen was immediately impressed with him. Standing well over six feet tall, and impeccably attired, he was a commanding figure from his blond hair to his icy blue eyes. Compared to the young men who constantly clamored for her attention, he seemed sophisticated and worldly. Although his taste in women did not generally include debutantes, he was immediately struck by the tall, beautiful redhead. He queried Robert Marlow, who was standing nearby.

"Who is the veritable goddess who has come to grace the season, my boy?" he inquired.

Robert was torn between keeping Kathleen away from Lord Ramsdale, and having the chance to expound on her many virtues.

"'Tis Lady Montgomery's granddaughter, the Lady Kathleen Malloy," he replied. "She is new come from Ireland." He stopped abruptly.

"Do present me, I beg you," Lord Ramsdale said, for he had not missed the hesitation in Robert's manner. Anything that made any of

Giles Brentwood's relatives uneasy must certainly be cultivated.

He had soon acquired a dance with Kathleen and made it a point to escort her to supper, carrying her off in the face of a disgruntled and angry Robert who had been planning on this *tête-à-tête* all evening. Robert's face was enough to please Lord Ramsdale, but in truth he was soon intrigued with Kathleen for her own sake. Her wit was quick, she had a delightful smile, and her beautiful face and figure commended her even to him, connoisseur that he was. It seemed pleasant not to have to stoop to some dainty miss; since she was tall, Kathleen's charms were more readily apparent. He kept the conversation light and did not seek her out after supper.

The next morning, however, a large bouquet of flowers arrived, bearing a card inscribed, "Hail, Persephone, daughter of Zeus!" It was unsigned, but both Kathleen and Lady Montgomery suspected Lord Ramsdale was the donor.

"Persephone, indeed!" Lady Montgomery snorted as they sat together over a late breakfast. "It is all very well, my girl, to count him a conquest, but I beg you to be careful. John Ramsdale has been on the London scene forever. His breeding is excellent, but his reputation is not too nice. There have been duels, and he had to spend some time abroad. He has been married before to an heiress who disappeared to the country soon after the wedding, in ill

health, although Ramsdale certainly didn't
bother to join her there. She died shortly thereafter. And it seems to me I remember a few
years back some altercation with Giles
Brentwood. It was hushed up, so I do not know
the details, but one assumes there was a lady
in the case. They are polite enemies now, that
I do know."

Kathleen was intrigued. Giles had still not
appeared in London, and until he arrived, her
plans to humiliate him were impossible. In
spite of her busy social life, she still found
herself dreaming of him, and it was certainly
frustrating to put off her plans of revenge for
so long.

Unknown to her, the duke was even then
being welcomed by his butler at Haven House,
his London establishment. He called for refreshment after his long ride and strolled to his
study, leaving the hall a scene of activity as his
servants removed his baggage and hastened to
comply with his wishes. Casting down his
gloves and riding crop on the mahogany desk
and warming his hands at the cheerful fire
prepared to welcome him, he was not surprised
to see his secretary enter with a salver piled
high with notes, invitations, and cards.

Smiling at this young man, he remarked,
"My dear Mark! What have we here? Barely in
the house five minutes, and you arrive to
badger me with business!"

Mark Fleming protested. "Your Grace, if I do
not catch you now, the next thing I know you

will be off to your clubs, and there are many items here that require your attention."

Giles eyed the pile uneasily as he accepted a glass of Madeira from the footman.

"I doubt if the clubs will see me for a week, for it appears that all London has been at the door, dear boy. Surely you know what invitations I will accept, and which must be consigned to the fire."

"Oh, I have already done that, m'lord. For example, I took the liberty of informing Lady Wells that it would be impossible for you to attend her masquerade on Tuesday next."

Mark Fleming smiled at the slight shudder Giles gave. He was only too aware that the duke despised Lady Wells, who had been trying, in a very vulgar way, to foist one of her innumerable daughters onto him for years.

"Quite right, quite right! I do not know what I would do without you, Mark! If I recall the Wells—hmmm—freckles, and would you say just the suspicion, one can only call it, of plumpness?"

Mark smiled. "Yes, m'lord, you have it. With all five young ladies, I believe."

The next half hour passed quickly as the duke decided which events he would attend. At one card he paused.

" 'Lady Montgomery requests the honor of my company at a ball . . . Friday evening . . . to present her granddaughter, Lady Kathleen,' " he read aloud. "Well, here's a mystery."

Mark told him as much as he knew about

the young lady and the circumstances of her being in London. The duke decided to attend. A granddaughter who had never been seen or spoken of for so many years was decidedly interesting, and in a vague way he seemed to remember the story. Kathleen would have been indignant if she had known how thoroughly she had been forgotten.

After disposing of business, and changing to town clothes, Giles set off on foot for White's. In a matter of hours the polite world would know the Duke of Havenhall had arrived back in town. His cousin Robert looked up as he entered the club.

"Giles!" he exclaimed, pumping his hand gladly. "Where have you been this age?"

"Surely London is not that much of a desert, my dear boy! You behold me finally in attendance, and I require you to give me all the latest gossip and *crim cons*. Who is here, who is there, who is together here and there!"

Robert happily complied. He told Giles that Lord Ramsdale was in town, which drew a slight frown, he mentioned various other friends, and then, ingenuously, he mentioned the matter nearest his heart.

"Giles, we have a goddess on the London scene this season! She has even been nicknamed 'goddess' by Lord Ramsdale!"

"A goddess?" queried Giles. "I have been away too long, it seems. Who is this paragon? Not one of the current crop of debutantes, of course. I assume this, since debs are hardly in Lord Ramsdale's usual style."

"Well, yes, Giles, she is in her first season. A veritable toast—of a beauty unparalleled—and you know her!" Robert teased.

"*I* know her? Surely I would remember such unrivaled beauty as you describe, unless six and twenty years are beginning to dim my wits!"

"'Tis Lady Kathleen, Lady Montgomery's granddaughter," Robert began.

Giles interrupted him with a languid wave of his hand.

"And how could I know the lady when she has been an enigma for so many years?"

Robert was enjoying himself, although he had an uneasy feeling about even mentioning Kathleen to his cousin. Giles invariably captured all too many hearts, and Robert felt he had enough competition as it was.

"Ah, but you have met the lady, at her home in Ireland. There she was Lady Kathleen Mary Malloy. And how did the Irish horses work out? Were you pleased?"

Giles frowned, remembering. "You mean that very tall young lady with the red hair and the magnificent stallion? Wonder of wonders! Well, you did say she would be the toast of London! I cry pardon, Robert! You were more farseeing than I, but I must certainly check this myself. Do you attend Lady Montgomery's ball? I shall make it a point to be presented to your goddess again at that happy event."

CHAPTER VII

(Lady Montgomery's Ball)

In the days that followed, Giles had the opportunity to see Kathleen only once, and that from a distance. For some reason their paths did not cross at the various parties they both attended. If Kathleen accepted an invitation to a Venetian breakfast, that was the morning the Duke of Havenhall joined a party of friends on a riding expedition. At Lady Booth's rout, none of Kathleen's partners were tall, dark, and superior, because that gentleman was playing deep basset with friends of long standing at his club. She might look for him in vain at Almack's, that was not one of his favorite haunts; and if she visited the libraries on Bond Street, he was probably sparring with Gentleman Jim that morning or visiting his tailor. He did, however, catch a glimpse of her in the park one afternoon while riding with Robert. She was as striking as ever, and her superior horsemanship drew many eyes. Robert sighed as he caught sight of her.

"There she is with that infernal Ramsdale again!" he exclaimed. Giles allowed a small crease of annoyance to appear on his otherwise expressionless face.

"So, the wind lies in that quarter, does it, dear boy?" he asked idly enough. "One hopes the lady has a firm head on her shoulders. Association with Lord Ramsdale can sometimes lead to—one can only say—unfortunate events for all concerned. With the exception of my dear Lord Ramsdale, of course."

"I like it no better than you, Giles. In fact, I mentioned it to Lady Montgomery the other day. I fear her head has been turned by all the attention her granddaughter is receiving, for she merely smiled and told me I was jealous! Since Kathleen was approved by the Beau, and all London calls her 'the goddess,' Lady Montgomery appears besotted with her success!"

Giles shrugged. "I begin to look forward to Lady Montgomery's ball with great anticipation," he admitted. "One does not like to be behind in the mode, and I can see that Lady Kathleen is definitely *à la mode* right now."

No one looked forward to that magical evening more than Lady Kathleen herself. She knew the Duke of Havenhall had arrived in London and had accepted his invitation to the ball, and she had spotted him herself that day in the park. Her heart beat oddly for a moment or two when she realized who the tall dark gentleman with Robert Marlow was, and Lord Ramsdale must have wondered at her sudden animation and glowing eyes when she turned her attention to him again. She was disap-

pointed that she was still riding her mare.
After a long pleading-session with her grandmother in which the name of Beau Brummel
figured prominently, she had been allowed to
send for Diablo, but it would be a while before
the stallion could be transported to town. Indeed, she had no notion how he was to get
there, but based her hopes on her pleas to her
father not to fail her in this, for it was
monstrous important that she have Diablo with
her.

Her grandmother had spent much time and
thought on Kathleen's attire for the ball that
would mark her very own come-out. For weeks
the house had been in an upset as caterers and
florists, musicians and *modistes* had made their
appearances. Kathleen offered to help when
she saw how much work there was, but her
grandmother, looking harassed, had bade her to
forget everything but her own plans, and when
Kathleen realized how very happy all the fuss
and bother made the old lady, she did not try
to assist her again. One would think that such
an upset to ordinary routine would tire an
elderly lady, but Lady Montgomery reveled in
it, and could be heard calling Bright and the
other staff members at all hours of the day.

The ballroom of the Eaton Square house was
a spacious chamber lit not only by several
chandeliers but also by elaborate wall sconces.
Its general decor was a pale yellow trimmed
with white and gold, and for several horrible
days both Kathleen and the staff felt that

Lady Montgomery would decide to have it completely redecorated, for she kept remarking that yellow was an insipid color. However, on being shown a gown of cloth of gold one afternoon at Madame Daphne's establishment, she exclaimed,

"The very thing! It will go prodigious well with the decor of the ballroom, and although many will say it is not quite the thing for a debutante, let 'em! You will look superb, my love, with your hair dressed *à la greque* and only the Montgomery pearls as adornment."

Kathleen sighed in relief. She had seen so many gowns, she really didn't care which one was chosen, they were all beautiful. On the evening of the ball, however, as she stood before her mirror while an excited Clara and a superior Griffin added the final touches and her grandmother made several suggestions, some of them contradictory, she was glad this particular gown had been chosen. The thin gold material flowed over her shoulders with fluid ease and was caught beneath her breasts with a braid of gold ribbon entwined with pearls. From there, it clung to her body or swirled away as she moved, catching the light. Her hair was entwined with golden ribbons and dressed regally, with nary a fussy curl to be seen. Around her neck she wore the promised Montgomery pearls which ended in the deep cleft between her breasts in a single amethyst, the final touch, Lady Montgomery declared. Long white kid gloves and flat gold slippers completed her outfit, and as she descended the stairs, Bright thought she looked like a golden angel, and her grandmother was sure no one would scoff at the title "goddess" after tonight. The excitement brought a flush to her cheeks and a sparkle to her eyes.

She carried no flowers in her tightly gloved hands. Indeed there were too many to choose from, so her grandmother had had them massed on a table behind her as they received the guests. There were Robert's pink blooms (such an unfortunate choice), and Lord Ramsdale's long-stemmed white roses, along with a host of other offerings. As Kathleen inspected the flowers and cards, her grandmother counted the titles assembled on them and she smiled. Four lords, a marquess, a duke, and assorted honorables. Very good!

Kathleen's eyes glowed with delight, and she gave her grandmother a hug which threatened the lady's purple plumes.

"Oh, my dear ma'am," she breathed. "It has all come true! How can I ever thank you for helping me?"

Her grandmother's eyes were wet, and she sought her handkerchief.

"Nonsense, gel! You refine too much on it!"

But in her heart she was reminded of her daughter Evelyn and wished she might be here to share her triumph. Before she became too choked up, she remembered that if Evelyn were alive, she probably would never have seen Kathleen at all, for she would still be buried on that farm with THAT MAN. Such thoughts quickly allowed her to regain her composure as the first guests were announced.

The ball was discussed by all the polite world for many days. Had you noticed the Beau's expression when he made his bow to Lady Kathleen? No one could know that the word he murmured to her as he kissed her hand was "superb!" And did you see the look in Lord Ramsdale's eyes when he first saw the lady in that revealing gown? My dear, they widened and then narrowed in a most sinister way! Of course it is no wonder, whatever was her grandmother thinking of to choose such a . . . such a provocative ensemble? I blushed when I saw her, truly blushed! No daughter of mine would ever . . . (Kathleen blushed too at Lord Ramsdale's comment, for he said, in a low voice, "Persephone herself! But more lovely!") And Robert Marlow! My dear, for all that the lady treats him like a younger brother, and teases him unmercifully, he was so enchanted with her, he could do nothing but stammer! One wonders, however, why she appeared to take such a dislike to Giles Brentwood? I did not think they had ever been introduced, but I was quite near when he was presented, and she turned positively pale. And then she spoke in such a cold putting-off way! You know, my dear, I have often called her much too coming, but no one could say so then. He noticed at once, of course, for his eyebrows rose alarmingly. He did, however, solicit her hand for a dance—it was one of the few times she appeared to advantage on the floor all evening. He is so much taller than even Lady Kathleen she looked positively fragile in his arms. What did you say? Oh, yes, and with Lord Ramsdale too! The duchess of Axminster, to whom these remarks had been addressed, snorted. She had had to watch her son, while dancing dutifully with his sister Jane, ogling Kathleen the entire time.

Truth be told, Kathleen was nervous as she watched Giles approach. She was aware that her coldness, over which she seemed to have no control, had surprised him, and she was afraid it had driven him away. But here he was, bowing before her with a dark smile which turned her heart over in her breast as he requested her company in the dance.

"For you know, m'lady," he said as he led her to the floor, "we are in the way of being old acquaintances. I hope you have not forgotten our meeting at Evelon Farm?"

Kathleen smiled at him politely, but underneath she seethed with anger. Forget, indeed! Oh, no, my dear duke, *I* have not forgotten! I wonder if you think I am "perfect for my setting" tonight? With her anger to steady her, she was able to give at least the appearance of charm and vivacity. So much so that Giles was intrigued. He had seldom seen a more beautiful girl, now he discovered her wit and intelligence. They were chatting still when the dance was over, and Lord Ramsdale did not look at all pleased as he came to claim her for the next dance. Giles stiffened slightly at his approach, and then drawled,

"My dear, *dear* Lord Ramsdale! I would say how glad I am to see you again except I perceive you are come to take the Lady Kathleen away, just as we were beginning to get reacquainted, which is so unkind of you!"

Kathleen glanced at both men in astonishment as Lord Ramsdale made him a mock bow, his lips thin with anger. There was something between them, to be sure!

"Come, Persephone!" he commanded. "You are promised to me!"

"Surely not Persephone," Giles remarked languidly. "I should rather call her 'Diana,' or perhaps 'Heliodora'—but you will have to check the reference yourself."

With a bow and a smile for Kathleen, he wandered away, soon to join the other gentlemen who were not dancing, in the card room. With a frown Lord Ramsdale watched him depart, and Kathleen put her hand on his arm.

"M'lord!" she commanded, "surely even a goddess is allowed a cold drink. I swear I am parched!"

He smiled down at her. "Why, goddess, I will hasten to comply, but I fear there is very little nectar here tonight, and that is the only thing you should allow to touch your lips!" As he spoke his eyes brushed her lips in a visible caress, and she hastened to turn and exclaim, "Nectar, indeed! Water would be nectar to me now!"

Giles did not ask her to dance again, and she was disappointed. She had felt strangely breathless when she was so close to him, and so she knew she had not handled the situation as well as she might have. She did not notice his eyes following her several times, or she might have been relieved. His attention was definitely caught by this tall, laughing girl in gold, with her beautiful face and stunning red hair. He observed her joking with Robert and several other young sprigs of fashion, and was less pleased when he saw Lord Ramsdale bend over her in a proprietary way. The Beau observed him.

"My dear Giles, are you to be caught in the damsel's coils too? I fear John Ramsdale has definitely succumbed this evening."

"She is certainly beautiful, and I would not like to see her in *his* coils!" he replied. "Did you know that Robert and I met her in Ireland this summer past when we went to her father's farm to purchase horses? My grays, you know you admired them, came from Evelon. Robert was more farseeing; he claimed then she would take London by storm, but I was sure it could never happen. She was so gauche and unsophisticated! More like a son than a daughter. Her grandmother is to be commended for this

Kathleen 91

vision we see tonight. A short while ago she wore breeches, tied her hair back with a thong, walked like a man, and even helped to deliver colts!"

Beau Brummel shuddered, but his thoughts were busy. He had observed the meeting between Giles and the goddess, and her coolness had intrigued him. Perhaps she had heard his friend's comments to Robert about her? It would be interesting to see the play develop, he thought as he strolled away, and perhaps the *dénouement* would also be amusing.

Although Giles was fascinated by the lady, he had been on the London scene too long to lose his head over a debutante, even one as handsome as Kathleen. He watched her dancing yet again with John Ramsdale, and his eyes narrowed. It had been many years since the unfortunate encounter that had engendered the two men's dislike, but there was still no love lost between them. A slight matter of Lord Ramsdale and a cousin of Giles; a pretty, ingenuous girl in her first season, who had fallen hard for the polished smoothness and charm of Lord Ramsdale, to the point where she forgot herself and imagined that love did indeed conquer all, and that to be together with her lover was all that mattered, without the benefit of matrimony, for his wife was at that time still sickly. Giles had been forced to intervene. What had happened between the two men, no one knew, but Ramsdale left very shortly on an extended tour of the Continent,

and the pretty cousin retired to her father's
country estate. Unfortunately, she never recovered from her infatuation. She had never
married; indeed her reputation had suffered
so, it was doubtful that anyone would have
offered for her, but she had since become
decidedly deranged. Perhaps she had expected
Ramsdale to come and claim her when his wife
died; he had not. It was something that a man
like Giles would not forget, or forgive. He was
not stuffed up with pride, but as head of the
family, and Duke of Havenhall, he knew his
consequence and his responsibility. Perhaps, he
mused, he had another opportunity to do his
dear, dear friend a disservice. Lord Ramsdale
was certainly enamored with the Lady Kathleen—perhaps he could charm the lady away
from danger, insuring her safety and his own
satisfaction as well. He smiled to himself, and
Robert Marlow, who was approaching, was
struck by that glinting smile that did not quite
reach the cold, narrowed eyes.

"Giles, there is something that amuses you?
I wish I could feel some amusement at the
moment! Look at Lord Ramsdale! I swear he
positively monopolizes Lady Kathleen! It is too
bad!"

Giles interrupted this tirade gently. "My
dear Robert, the lady has the choice as
always." He smoothed a wrinkle in his dove
gray satin sleeve. "That is the way of the
world. However, the gentle sex has often been
known to change its mind. Perhaps that will

occur in this case."

Robert brightened at the thought, not knowing that Giles meant to turn her attention to himself. The two cousins leisurely made their way from the ballroom, Robert still expostulating on Kathleen's beauty, wit, and grace.

As that lady wended her way to bed in the early hours that the ball finally concluded, she was weary but happy. The ball had been a success, and she had had a wonderful time, and the duke of Havenhall was finally within her grasp; well, at least within the reach of her grasp, she thought sleepily. She only wished her father and the boys could have been there to see her. Ireland seemed so very far away now.

CHAPTER VIII

(Lord Ramsdale Decides)

Lady Montgomery had every reason to be pleased with her granddaughter's debut. The ball had gone smoothly with none of the contretemps that sometimes marred other occasions. There had been plenty of excellent champagne and various punches, the jellies and pastries had been of the first quality, and the lobster patties had not disappeared too quickly. The music had been good; not too loud, yet almost continuous, and Bright had kept a firm hand on the extra servants hired for the occasion. No one had spilled a tray of champagne on some starchy dowager, and not one debutante had dissolved in tears and had to be soothed by her mama in the ladies' withdrawing room—an event that had occurred many times before. All the world had been there to see Lady Montgomery's triumph, and she was more than pleased with Kathleen; she had been everything she ought and more. When she considered the miracle she had wrought with the girl, and in such a short time, she puffed up with pride. Drinking her morning chocolate, the lady was decidedly satisfied.

She reviewed once again the evening's events, and the only cloud on her horizon was Lord Ramsdale's excessive attentions to Kathleen. She had only granted him two dances, which was correct, but wherever she seemed to be during the evening, he was *there*. She resolved to speak to Kathleen about this again. No sense in letting it go too far, and a connection with a peer with a decidedly soiled reputation was not what she wished at all. Not, she added mentally, with a perfectly good Duke of Havenhall in the offing. She had observed Giles very carefully and felt his attention had been piqued by her granddaughter. If only this attraction could be strengthened somehow, but very carefully! 'Ware hurry! She must be extremely devious to trick Giles, she knew, but she felt more than equal to the task. At the moment there was nothing to be done. She summoned Griffin and began to dress for the day. When she was finally attired to her dresser's satisfaction, she made her way to the front hall to confer with Bright. It was pleasant to see the many cards and flowers that had already been delivered to her and Kathleen, but her eyes opened wide when she beheld Giles Brentwood being ushered into the hall.

"Good morning, ma'am!" this gentleman said, making her an elegant bow. "My compliments on a splendid evening. I am sure you are happy with the results."

Lady Montgomery wondered, not for the first time, why Giles always managed to see straight to the heart of the matter, and then speak it plainly, but all she said as she extended her hand was, "Well, Giles, and whatever are you doing here? I have not seen you this age, and suddenly you are in my house two days in succession." Leading the way to the morning room, she added, "Surely you are not come to add a bouquet to my granddaughter's collection!"

Giles smiled as he waited for the lady to seat herself.

"And why not?" he queried gently. "I perceived last night that the Lady Kathleen is to be the 'Incomparable of the Incomparables' this season. Of course I must pay my homage to the lady. Would you have me remiss in any little courtesy to the season's brightest star?"

Lady Montgomery lowered her eyes, for she was thinking hard. What roundabout was this? After one dance, Giles had ignored Kathleen the rest of the evening.

Giles continued. "I was wondering if the lady would be free to drive in the park with me this afternoon. I have brought the horses I purchased from her father to London, and would like her to see them in action."

Lady Montgomery arranged her shawl carefully. "Why, as to that, I have no idea whether my granddaughter is free this afternoon. I shall inquire."

She rang the bell for Bright and sent a message to Kathleen's room, that lady not having made an appearance this morning.

Then the two chatted desultorily of this and that. Although two generations apart, their families had been acquainted forever.

How like his father he is! she thought as she watched his tall, rangy form lounging against the mantle. The same dark, smooth hair, the same dark gray eyes that let you see only as much as he himself wished, the elegant hands, and the smoothly muscled legs that managed to look powerful even in the morning dress suitable to a gentleman caller. Truly an elegant man, but no fop; a man in every sense. She resolved again to bring him to heel for Kathleen.

Bright reported that the Lady Kathleen would be delighted to join the Duke of Havenhall for a drive in the park at four that afternoon, and Giles took himself off, declining all offers of refreshment.

Kathleen was still above stairs when Lord Ramsdale, the next caller, appeared. He was disappointed that he had to make his compliments in absentia, and since Lady Montgomery did not feel she had to press a glass of Madeira on him, he soon found himself strolling to his club. He thought again of the Lady Kathleen as he walked along. He had not seen her like for many a day, and he was determined to have her, one way or the other. He was surprised when he realized that that included matrimony, if that were the only way. The Irish connection was deplorable, of course, but it was more than balanced by the Montgomery

side of the family, and the lady's beautiful self.
There was probably not much money there,
unless Lady Montgomery decided to leave her
something, but since Lord Ramsdale's late wife
had left him extremely rich in his own right,
this did not weigh with him. He knew from a
conversation at the ball last evening that Kathleen would be at the theater tonight with a
party of friends, and decided the play would
certainly have his patronage too.

That afternoon, promptly at the hour ap-
pointed, Giles tooled his curricle and new team
to the front door of Montgomery House. His
tiger leaped for the horses' heads, and Giles
ascended the steps. Bright admitted him, and
a footman was sent to notify Lady Kathleen.
No waiting about was neccessary, which Giles
had known, for this lady was well aware that
it did not do to keep spirited horses standing,
and she soon swept down the stairs, already
bonneted and cloaked for the drive. Giles observed her critically. She was a beautiful girl,
to be sure, and her excitement at taking a
drive with her sworn enemy, added to the
chance to see her father's horses again, had
brought a gentle rose to her cheeks and a
sparkle to her eyes. She was dressed in a deep
violet walking dress which seemed to match
her blue eyes. Her bonnet was severe enough
not to detract from the glorious chestnut curls
that peeped from beneath it. Drawing on her
tight violet kid gloves, she said,

"I am ready, sir, as you see."

"In good time, m'lady," he replied. "I knew that you would not keep me waiting when there were horses to be considered."

As he escorted her down the steps, Lady Kathleen pondered.

"Do you have such a poor opinion of my sex, Your Grace?" she queried, looking up at him from under her dark lashes. "I must admit that I am invariably early for everything. I have never cultivated the polite world's habit of lateness for the sake of fashion."

She broke off as she spied the horses being attended by the groom, and hastened to their heads. The groom was alarmed when the young miss reached up to them—High bred 'uns, and snappish still in the bustle of town, he thought. He made a move to stop her, but the duke halted him effectively with a raised hand, and watched the lady as she greeted her old friends.

"Well, Smoke; my dear Gray Star! Are you behaving yourselves? And are you giving the duke a comfortable ride? It is so good to see you again!"

As she stood stroking the velvet noses, the groom was amazed to see his "high bred 'uns" positively sidling and whinnying to her. He felt he could drop the bridle, and neither horse would move unless it were closer to the lady. Strange, indeed. Kathleen recalled herself and smiled at him before she returned to the duke and allowed him to assist her to the high seat. As Giles gave his horses the office to start, and the groom jumped up behind, Kathleen exclaimed,

"Oh, they are like a breath of home! And as beautiful as I remembered!"

She watched the duke's strong hands control the reins effortlessly, although she was well aware what strength was required for such prize horseflesh, especially since they had not settled down to the London traffic and confusion. With ease, the duke did not let them take exception to a hackney coach coming from the opposite direction, or a flower seller's cries, which seemed to annoy them. Kathleen had remained silent, as had the duke, until the more open ways of the park were reached. With scarcely a check, they swept through the gates, and she exclaimed,

"How well you drive, sir! I know it is not easy to handle Smoke, especially—he *will* take advantage if he can, but it is merely high spirits, there's no vice in him at all."

The duke was amused. "Why, I thank you, m'lady! I am generally said to have a fairly good hand."

Kathleen blushed. She recalled that Giles was top of the trees, a nonpareil, and one of the Four Horse Club, whose members were among the best drivers in London. Robert had told her, adding that not even the fact that he was Giles' cousin could gain him admittance to that select group. Before she could redeem herself, the duke continued with a warm smile,

"But praise from you is always welcome. I

know your expertise with horses. I have seen you ride, remember!"

Kathleen's chin rose slightly. The duke was not going to forget her origins, or let her forget he knew of them. When she remembered how she had been dressed that morning in Ireland, she was mortified. A little flame of anger flickered in the back of her mind. Oh, it would be good to bring this haughty nobleman to his knees! But she composed her features in a smile and nodded to him.

"Why, to be sure, so you do. I must say that delightful as London is, I do miss a good gallop! You must know how sedately a lady is supposed to ride."

"It must be irksome," Giles replied, "especially since you are wont to ride astride. I imagine you also miss your beautiful stallion. Have you any news of him?"

As he spoke, Giles turned his head to look directly at the lady and was surprised to see the flashing of her eyes. He could have sworn she was angry, but what on earth had he said to provoke her? The dark lashes dropped swiftly over those telltale eyes as she answered him.

"I hope to have news of him shortly. I have written to my father asking him to send Diablo to London."

Giles chuckled, in spite of his momentary confusion, as a thought occurred to him.

"And how did you get around Lady Montgomery, I wonder? I wager she does not approve of her granddaughter riding a stallion in polite society."

Kathleen dimpled. "Indeed, Your Grace, it was prodigious hard to get her to agree, even though the Beau suggested it to me."

"Aha! That explains it! When Brummel speaks, even your grandmother attends, I know. You must let me have the honor of escorting you when you make your first appearance on Diablo. I suppose the Beau told you to wear black? Yes, of course, nothing but black velvet would do to complete the picture!"

"How did you guess? Perhaps a little white lace, do you think?" Kathleen was bubbling with laughter inside.

He stole another glance at her face and was enchanted with the deep dimple beside her mouth. The lady was volatile; one moment stormy, the next amused, an intriguing combination.

"Oh, definitely white lace," was all he said in agreement, however.

They continued to chat of horses and the London scene as they swept around the park. Many of the fashionable world observed them that afternoon, including Robert Marlow who was dutifully escorting his grandmother in her barouche. That redoubtable lady poked him with her parasol as he stared at Giles and Kathleen when they drove by the slower-moving carriage with friendly smiles.

"So, that's the lie of the land, is it!" she exclaimed. "Best you choose some other lady to dangle after. With the duke and John Ramsdale in contention for the lady's favors, you are quite beside the pale!" Mrs. Marlow chuckled at his discomfiture.

John Ramsdale did not have the felicity to observe the stunning couple, but his friend Captain Cranshaw informed him of it that evening as they were driving in to the theater. Ramsdale's eyes darkened in annoyance. Giles Brentwood had better be extremely wary. He would brook no interference in his plans for the lady, and those plans did not include the honorable Duke of Havenhall. In their last encounter he was aware he had come off second best, but this time he was confident of his success. It would be a pleasure to put Giles in his place and sweep the lady away from under his nose. Since his wife had finally succumbed to her illness, there was no need of the tactics he had used with Giles' cousin. Marriage it would be, and he had every intention of making haste to gain the lady's hand before that damned duke attracted her fancy. He observed the lady and her party in their box from the floor of the theater, but since the box was crowded with friends, he did nothing more than wave gently when she looked his way. He determined to present himself at the first interval.

When he entered the box, he was well aware

of Lady Montgomery's stiffness, although she was bound to be gracious. He greeted the lady and then turned slightly to whisper to Kathleen,

"You were a vision in gold last evening, m'lady. One would say it would be hard to improve on such loveliness, yet here you are, radiant in white! Can it be to honor my flowers you chose white?"

Kathleen was confused, for Lord Ramsdale had brought more white roses to the house that morning. How dare he assume such a thing? She was startled as she looked up at him. Those blue eyes were not icy now! In fact there was such passion and lust in his glance as his eyes swept her bare shoulders and half-concealed breasts that she was alarmed and drew back slightly. It took a moment before she regained her composure and was able to answer.

"Why, no such thing, m'lord! The gown is new and my grandmother asked me to wear it this evening. 'Twas only the thought of pleasing her, I do assure you!"

Ramsdale decided to retreat. He had not missed the fright in those magnificent eyes. Meekly he said,

"To be sure. Forgive me! I spoke without thinking, but goddesses must get used to being admired by their adoring subjects."

Kathleen raised her head and looked at him directly.

"M'lord, I beg you to forget that silly *sobriquet*. It upsets me, and I do not think it is at all the thing!"

"It shall be as you wish," the gentlemen replied smoothly. "I beg you not to refine on it too much. I can see you are upset, so I will leave you now."

He bowed formally and took his leave, and Lady Montgomery drew a breath of relief. She had not heard the words exchanged, but she was aware that Kathleen had rebuked John Ramsdale, and she was pleased. He did not reappear that evening, for which Kathleen was grateful. My lord Ramsdale went too far, and too fast, to please her, and it was no part of her plan to have him desiring her so obviously when she was intent on snaring the Duke of Havenhall. She had hoped to use him to pique the duke's interest, but if that course was no longer open to her, she would have to contrive something else. Lord Ramsdale was aware that he had made a slip by becoming too ardent, too soon. She was, for all her beauty, merely a young girl, and he had rushed her. An older woman, as he knew well from experience, would have known how to handle the flirtation. He would retire momentarily, but he would enter the lists again, as soon as the lady's anger had cooled.

In the days that followed, he made no move to seek her out, merely bowing to her when they met, although the morning after the

theater party he had sent a small nosegay of
white rosebuds and an abject apology for
disturbing her. It was so nicely phrased that
she was reassured, and when he took himself
off to his country estate for a few days to give
her time to recover, she soon forgot her fright
and anger at him. Giles Brentwood was in-
creasingly attentive, although he made no
move to single her out too often, and seemed to
derive a great deal of amusement from her
beaus. She wondered what to do next. At a
ball, in the park, at a cotillion, he was
pleasant, and he always asked for a dance, but
he moved no closer.

It was her habit now, when she attended any
party, to immediately scan the guests to see if
the duke were present. She was astonished to
spot him at Lady Morgan's musical evening
since he hardly seemed the type to sit on little
gilt chairs enjoying the classics as presented by
a group of amateurs. Lady Montgomery informed her that the duke was a relation of
Lady Morgan's, which somewhat explained it.
Kathleen was feeling distinctly uneasy, since
she had been requested to bring her music, and
her grandmother had insisted she do so.

After an intermission for wine and cakes,
Lady Axminster led her daughter Jane, coyly
protesting to the harp. Kathleen exchanged a
glance with Giles, seated some little distance
away from her. He raised his eyes to heaven
briefly, and Kathleen had to smile in return.

Jane intercepted the glances as she was making much of settling herself at the instrument. She flushed angrily, determined to best this arrogant nobody with the red hair if she could.

After several selections which she performed most creditably, since she had a genuine musical talent, she refused to play another encore. Instead she indicated Kathleen and said,

"But surely we should listen to the Lady Kathleen now! Perhaps she will favor us with a selection on the harp or pianoforte."

Kathleen sank back in her chair, but to no avail, for her grandmother firmly propelled her forward.

She faced the audience and said softly,

"I am afraid I have no skill on either instrument and would hate to have to follow such an accomplished performance as we have just heard. However, if an accompanist can be found, I will do my best to sing for you."

There was applause, and a young pianist came forward. Too soon Kathleen found herself in a situation she had been dreading since she left Greywood. After a shaky start, she managed to complete the aria without error, but it was an uninspired performance. Over the polite applause that followed, Giles heard Lady Jane titter to her neighbor,

"What a shame she is so badly trained! I would never have consented to perform if I couldn't do better than that!"

The duke felt unreasonable annoyance, so he called out,

"Lady Kathleen! Perhaps you would sing us something of your own choosing?"

Several gentlemen gamely seconded the request. Kathleen conferred with the pianist, who shook his head. She turned to the audience and announced that she would like to sing an Irish folk song, but it would have to be *a cappella,* since there was no music for the pianist.

The room hushed and she began. Suddenly all her restraint and hesitancy vanished as she sang of the land and the people she loved. It was a simple song she had learned as a child, and the pianist soon picked it up and accompanied her softly. And into that crowded, overheated room with its brilliant company came the hills and streams of Ireland, the peat fires and the sea, and all the loneliness a man or woman can feel, when far from home. Kathleen ended on a poignant minor note, her head bowed, and for several moments the room was deathly still. As she looked up in alarm, feeling her choice of song had been most unwise, the applause started and grew in enthusiasm, but although pressed, Kathleen would perform no more. Her grandmother squeezed her hand as she regained her seat. She had been horrified when Kathleen announced her second selection, but she saw now that it had been the perfect choice. She smiled triumphantly at the Duchess of Axminster, while everyone crowded around Kathleen to compliment her.

She soon found herself sipping a glass of wine, with the duke smiling down at her.

"Very beautifully performed, m'lady," he said. "I think you should leave the arias to others, and only sing of your homeland."

Kathleen, who had blushed at his opening words, now bristled angrily. Drat the man! Must he always twit her about Ireland? She bowed coldly and asked to be excused, puzzling the duke once again with her changeability.

CHAPTER IX

*(Concerning a Horse,
Two Brothers,
and One Lover)*

One morning shortly thereafter, an event occurred that drove music, the duke, Lord Ramsdale, and all the polite world right from Kathleen's mind. She came down the stairs, ready to accompany her grandmother on a shopping expedition, to find Bright ushering two tall young gentlemen with flaming red heads into the morning room. He looked bemused, so alike they were, and what Lady Montgomery was going to say to this he could only guess. It would not be to her liking, that he knew.

Kathleen ran down the remaining steps, exclaiming,

"Tony! George! Where have you come from? Oh, it has been an age since I saw you last!"

She fell into their arms, trying to kiss and hug them both together. The young men appeared embarrassed by this female display and tried to extricate themselves quickly.

"Have done, Katie Mary!" Tony finally exclaimed, putting her firmly from him. "Yes, we are here, and a long trip it has been too!"

George nodded in agreement. "And all for a whim of yours, my girl!" he said.

"My whim? And what has that to do, pray, with your appearing in London? Oh, how is Father, and the rest of the boys? And Evelon? Nothing is wrong there, is it?"

"Everything is fine, Katie Mary," Tony reassured her. "We are here at your bidding. Have you forgotten you asked Father to send you Diablo?"

George added, "And he decided it was time Tony and I had some town polish, so we brought him to town for you."

Kathleen whirled around to George.

"Diablo is here? Oh, how wonderful! Where is he? Did the trip upset him? Has he missed me?"

George raised his large hand. "Whoa, Katie Mary! One question at a time."

Tony said musingly, "Note how she shows more concern for the horse than for us, brother. Never mind if the trip upset *us!*"

George laughed. "That's no surprise!" he said, and then to Kathleen, he asked, "Perhaps we could sit down? It *has* been a long trip, and we stayed only to find an inn where we could put up before we came straight to you." Kathleen linked arms with them both and led them into the morning room, asking Bright to bring refreshments. The boys watched the butler with awe. To think their sister could speak so calmly and with such authority to such a paragon! And she looked prodigious elegant too in her morning dress of primrose muslin, with her hair done up in fashionable curls. They were suddenly shy, but she would have none of that!

"Yes, yes, I am a young lady of fashion, as you can see," she twinkled. "But it is the same Kathleen Mary underneath, and if you do not tell me immediately about Diablo, you will see some of my famous Malloy temper! I'm sure you remember that, even if you are not sure you remember me!"

Tony laughed and stretched luxuriously, more at ease now.

"Aye, we remember that all right! Father always said you had the worst temper of the lot of us! Diablo is in Lady Montgomery's stables. As we were bringing him here, we met a groom who told us how to get to the mews where the stables are. He seemed to know we were your brothers."

"I wonder why?" mused George, looking innocent.

"Oh, that is Fitton, Grandmother's head groom. I have told him all about Diablo, so perhaps he recognized the horse, and not just the red hair on your heads! As soon as you have had some wine, take me around to see him, please!"

Before the boys could agree, Bright appeared with a silver tray and decanter and glasses and was followed closely by Lady Montgomery. That lady was distinctly annoyed, but as the two young men jumped to their feet and bowed, her face softened. So tall and handsome they were! And as alike as two peas in a pod! However, she had no intention of putting them up and introducing them to society. As they talked, it became clear that that was the last thing they wanted. Their idea of a good time in London did not include balls, teas, shopping, and the theater; at least not the theaters that she and Kathleen frequented. They intended to have a high old time in London, and considered that in delivering Diablo, their duty was done. Now they could get on with the important business at hand: cockfights, boxing exhibitions, horse races, cards, and any number of low taverns complete with low company. Well, thought Lady Montgomery, it won't hurt them, and young men being what they were, she could only be grateful there were two of them so one could keep an eye on the other. Bailing them out of jail was not in her plans either. They were polite and presentable, and called her "Lady Montgomery," with never a "Grandmother" crossing their lips, and for their sakes that was just as well.

Kathleen begged her grandmother to be excused from the shopping trip so she could go to the stables to see her horse, and Lady Montgomery graciously agreed. In fact, she also agreed that Kathleen might have her brothers' escort when she rode in the park that afternoon. There was no hiding them, with those heads of hair, so they might as well be put to best advantage to serve Kathleen. What a three-some they would make!

The boys were not as enthusiastic as Kathleen, but they manfully agreed to postpone their plans for one afternoon, and a time was agreed to. Tony and George took themselves off thankfully. Katie Mary seemed to get along with the old lady all right, but the less they had to do with her, the better!

Diablo whinnied eagerly as he heard Kathleen's voice when she entered the stables a few minutes later.

"Fitton! Where is he? I can hardly wait to see my beauty again!"

The old groom wiped away a tear when he saw Kathleen put her arms around Diablo's neck. The horse bent down to her, for all the world like a person, so she could reach him, and whinnied with happiness as she stroked him. Several happy minutes later, she told Fitton to have him ready for four o'clock, for she was riding in the park with her brothers then.

Fitton had been hesitant when he saw the size of the stallion and had wondered if even Kathleen could control such a high bred 'un in the noisy London streets, but after witnessing their reunion, he knew she would have no trouble at all, and so, shortly before four, he himself brought the horse around to the front door, complete with the saddle that had accompanied his tack. He never noticed it was not a sidesaddle, for to his unconscious mind such an animal would naturally be equipped with a man's saddle.

Anthony and George were already waiting for Kathleen, and he paused to speak to them and admire their mounts. Tony rode a dark gray, and George a dapple gray, but neither could hold a candle to Diablo and Lady Kathleen when she jumped lightly into the saddle. They were a magnificent sight, the huge, shining black stallion and the tall girl dressed all in black velvet with only the promised Alençon lace foaming at her cuffs and throat to relieve the darkness. That, and of course her brilliant red hair. She wore it dressed severely, and her riding hat was severe too, almost a man's hunting cap. Fitton gasped. There was the lady riding astride! What a to-do there would be, and Lady Montgomery would blame him! He moved forward as Kathleen finished adjusting her black gloves and picked up the reins.

"M'lady, I beg of you! Do not go! You must have your sidesaddle! Lady Montgomery will kill me for sure if you ride astride!"

Kathleen's color heightened, the old groom was so upset.

"Nonsense, Fitton," she said briskly, "I am always wont to ride Diablo astride. I will explain to my grandmother when I return, and no blame will fall on you."

She moved Diablo forward before he could remonstrate with her again for riding this way in the city. It was just not done, no, nor in the country either! Young ladies of fashion had to

be careful not to offend the rules of polite
society, and he shook his head mournfully as
he contemplated the rumpus that this would
create, even as one side of him admired the
picture they made.

By the time the park gates were reached,
both Tony and George, as well as Kathleen
herself, were aware that perhaps she had gone
too far. Several ladies had snubbed her, after
their initial gasp of shock, and several gentlemen had ogled her to the point where Tony
had had to be restrained from riding back to
teach them a lesson. Kathleen kept her head
high, but there was a lump in the back of her
throat, and her hands quivered slightly on the
reins. Fortunately Diablo behaved beautifully,
ignoring all the provocations of the crowded
streets.

Inside the park, Kathleen drew a sigh of
relief. At least it wasn't as populated as the
street, and they could ride abreast. George
asked tentatively,

"Is it such a bad thing, then, Katie Mary, to
ride astride in town? Perhaps we shouldn't
have let you . . ."

Kathleen interrupted him, her head held
even higher as she saw the Countess of Derby
pointing her out to her companions.

"Well, perhaps it is not done much," she
agreed, well aware that only the vulgar on the
fringe of society did it to call attention to
themselves, and that common actress—what
was her name?—she had heard that she rode

astride too. "However, what do we care what they think? Let us canter; it has been an age since I rode this way. No racing though, boys! And no galloping, that I know is beyond the pale."

"Sad stuff," muttered Tony as he cantered sedately by her side.

Even if Kathleen had been conventionally dressed and saddled, she would still have attracted attention that golden afternoon. All society, it seemed, was walking or riding, exchanging *bon mots* and gossip, greeting their friends, and staring at the vision in black on the huge black stallion, attended by not one, but two, redheaded giants as handsome as she. As the threesome swept round the ride, Kathleen saw a high perch phaeton approaching, containing Beau Brummel, with Giles Brentwood at the reins. She drew up her horse on signal. The Beau was laughing, but the duke looked distinctly angry. His eyes narrowed in a frown as he stared at her, and his bow was exceedingly cool.

"Lady Kathleen, I protest!" the Beau exclaimed. "Now did I go so far as to mention a man's saddle? 'Pon rep, I swear I was not so bold! However, the effect, with your attendant twin Adonises is all that I pictured. Magnificent!"

Kathleen smiled at him tremulously, peeping at the duke under her lashes.

"I fear I have overstepped the bounds, sir,"

she replied. "Several people have snubbed me already . . ."

The duke interrupted her harshly.

"And more will assuredly do so! What a very stupid thing to do, m'lady. It does you no good to challenge society in this way!"

Tony cleared his throat, and the duke seemed to catch sight of the lady's escort for the first time. He raised his quizzing glass and eyed them intently. For some reason, George no longer liked the way his cravat was tied, and Tony was sure there was a smut on his face.

"You, no doubt," the duke said icily, "are the lady's brothers, new come from Ireland. I deduce that, since anyone who knows anything about town would have realized how disastrous this is for the Lady Kathleen."

Kathleen felt close to tears, but in spite of them glistening in her lashes, she replied before the boys could get a word out.

"May I present my brothers, sirs, the honorable Anthony and George Malloy. They are newly arrived, as you surmised, m'lord, but the blame is all mine. I, at least, knew the rules."

Before the duke could reply—and Brummel could tell that it would be a blistering retort from the set of his shoulders and the rigidness of his hands on the reins—that gentleman said,

"Come, come! Never apologize, m'lady. Since the damage . . . hmm . . . seems to be done, may I suggest that you carry it off in style? That is the only way you will succeed in this slightly . . . hmm . . . mad caper. Put your chin up, bow graciously to one and all, and try to appear as if nothing is out of the common way."

Kathleen smiled at him, albeit a trifle shakily.

"You are kind, sir! I shall take your advice, although 'twill be a hard thing to do."

The Beau signaled Giles to start. "You have already made a beginning toward acceptance, m'lady. Have not the great Giles Brentwood and Beau Brummel himself been speaking to you for several minutes? Off you go—at least twice around the park I think would be best, so none will think you vanquished—you can do it!"

With a friendly wave to the boys and a smile to Lady Kathleen, he settled back beside his friend and remarked as the trio rode away,

"Of course, it would have been helpful if the great Giles Brentwood had removed that sullen frown of disapproval."

The duke turned his head and raised one black eyebrow.

"Think you so, my friend? I admit to unreasonable anger."

"Of course, one wonders," the Beau remarked, bowing to the Marquess of Lambertshire, "what business it is of yours. You are not affianced to the chit that I have heard, nor even distantly related."

He ignored Giles' now-ferocious frown and smiled sweetly at a young debutante who went home in a whirl, sure her fortune was now made, for the Beau himself had smiled at her at last.

Beau Brummel enjoyed the remainder of his ride, certainly more than either Giles or Kathleen did. He even managed to put in a good word for her when the duke, at an imperious signal from the Duchess of Axminster, drew up beside that lady's barouche.

The duchess was all agog at what she had seen, and allowed her daughter Jane to get out only a short greeting before she asked if the gentlemen had seen that Irish chit . . . so coming! . . . it was hard to believe! . . . right here in Hyde Park! . . . what was the world coming to? . . . she still felt quite faint . . . if only she had not misplaced her vinaigrette . . . she herself had always said she did not think her at all the thing, Lady Montgomery or no . . .

The Beau languidly allowed her to run down before he replied smoothly. "Of course, it is too bad, m'lady, but it is common practice in Ireland, you know"—knowing full well the lady had as much knowledge of Ireland as he had himself, and that was very little. He continued, "Surely only a lady with such a magnificent seat could attempt it! I vow you will find the lady has set fashion, although I would hesitate to recommend it to any lady who was not a superb rider."

He gently adjusted his cuffs and smiled kindly at Jane whose expertise on the harp did not extend to her riding, and who was well known for her ham-handed handling of any horse she came in contact with. Jane returned the smile, but the duchess was horrified. Neither lady had any idea they were being mocked, and since the duchess suddenly found herself with very little to say, and Giles made few contributions, the encounter was soon terminated. Jane was sorry; she would have liked to have asked if those very handsome young gentlemen were related to the Lady Kathleen.

A few well chosen words in other ears that afternoon did much to smooth Kathleen's path when she appeared at a ball given by Lord and Lady Stanton that evening. She knew her grandmother would hear of her escapade, indeed she had entertained the thought of confessing it to her before her courage failed. As Lady Montgomery greeted an old friend, and that lady gave Kathleen a cold and distant stare, Kathleen felt it right down to the soles of her celestial blue slippers, but she smiled sweetly in return and kept her head high. Lady Montgomery would find no fault with her posture tonight!

It seemed to Kathleen that the throng of admirers had lessened, and although she was never without a partner, Giles Brentwood did not approach her, favoring her instead with a cold bow from across the room. When a young gentleman dared to squeeze her hand during a country dance and whisper, "M'lady! I don't care what anyone says! I think you were outstanding!" her cup of unhappiness overflowed. She knew her grandmother had heard all the details of the story by now, and dreaded the moment when she would be summoned to her side. Lady Montgomery, however, hid her distress very well when one of her dearest friends told her the whole as they sat watching the set now forming.

"My dear Eleanor, I grieve for you! After all you have done for the girl! It is such ingratitude that I swear I am overcome with pity for you!"

Lady Montgomery stiffened. Mary Emerson pity *her*? Her hands tightened on her fan, but she replied casually enough.

"Do not refine on it, dear Mary. In time it will be forgotten, next week there will be a new scandal for the gossips to chew over, and after all, the gel did nothing to put her outside the pale."

She looked up and saw Beau Brummel chatting gaily with her granddaughter and felt immeasurably better. Indeed she was less angry than Kathleen had any right to expect, but still a tide of reproach swept over her as they were driven home after the ball. Kathleen promised to behave herself, but when Lady Montgomery tried to make her promise never to do it again, she answered quickly,

"But Grandmother! Beau Brummel assured me that if I stopped, it would be worse! Now that I have ridden astride once, he says that I must make it my habit until people start taking it for granted."

"Never!" shrieked her grandmother. "Is he

out of his mind? I was delighted of course to see him talking to you, and I will inquire tomorrow as to the damage that has been done. Until I find out, shall we say no riding at all, my girl?"

Kathleen had to agree, and it was with a heavy heart that she allowed Clara to undress her and chatter as she did so. That young woman was already fearful that she would be dismissed as soon as Lady Montgomery heard of her indiscretion in dressing Lady Kathleen in her split riding skirt, and the scene with Griffin that had yet to take place she was not looking forward to at all! She knew the other servants would have the whole story in the morning and she knew she faced their combined wrath for letting their young lady make such a cake of herself, and just when things were going so well in the matrimonial lists. Griffin favored Lord Ramsdale, she had a weakness for blond hair and blue eyes, no matter what dark thoughts they covered, but Bright had put his heart on the Duke of Havenhall. He was somber when he greeted Lady Kathleen the following morning.

"Oh, no, Bright!" she exclaimed. "Was it so bad? I swear I did not realize and surely I have been punished enough without your disapproval too!"

Bright tried to smile at her, but so far there had been only one floral offering delivered that morning, and he feared the worst.

Into this turmoil reappeared Lord Ramsdale.

He heard of Lady Kathleen's escapade moments after he entered his club, delighted to be back in town after the boredom of the country. He chuckled when Chomledsly told him the whole, and made it a point to make his bow to Kathleen that evening.

With all the events that had taken place, Kathleen had forgotten that Lord Ramsdale had frightened her with his ardor that night at the theater. She was in fact glad to see him so attentive. Here at least was someone who did not disapprove of her, like Giles, and she managed a smile when he said that Diana was a more fitting *soubriquet* for her now.

"You are too good, m'lord! I fear London does not take kindly to such escapades by debutantes. The Duke of Havenhall quite took me to task!"

Lord Ramsdale laughed lightly. "Did he now? But that is not his place, surely? Or have I been absent too long?"

Kathleen swept him a curtsey as the dance ended and, smiling up at him, she was surprised to see how ardent he looked. Oh dear, she remembered now, and after she imagined she had taken care of that once and for all. A mask came over his face as he escorted her to her grandmother, and he was so correct in taking his leave, that she thought that she had perhaps misinterpreted that one, lover-like look in his eyes.

CHAPTER X

(The Wrong Proposal Is Declined)

Giles, in the meantime, had been amazed at the anger he had felt at Kathleen's daring. As Brummel had gently pointed out, what was it to him what she did? And yet, and yet . . . somehow it did matter! He retreated into himself at once and spent many an hour wondering why this should be so important to him. Now it was the great Duke of Havenhall's turn to mutter to himself at odd times, "silly chit!" and "why did I not point out to her?" or "after all, why do I care if she makes a fool of herself? She is nothing to me!"

His valet, Brown, eyed him strangely, and his butler took great care that no detail should be overlooked in the running of the house. Well he knew the signs; there was trouble brewing for someone, he merely intended to be sure that it did not have his name on it! Mark Fleming was sure that the duke was in love, and he wondered which pretty little light skirt it was this time. He sincerely hoped she would not be as expensive as the last, and would not treat the duke to as many unpleasant scenes. He tried to avoid bothering him with petty

details and felt a great deal of sympathy for
him. Some might say the duke was starched up
and proud, Mark knew differently.

Robert Marlow was also taken aback by
Kathleen's escapade. He had not seen her in
the park and had had the story from several
different sources, with the usual results. His
heart ached for her, although if the truth be
told, he was faintly shocked, for what was all
right on an Irish horse farm could not be
admired in town. He was really a very conven-
tional young man, and he had put Kathleen on
such a pedestal that it was hard for him to
accept even the slightest misdemeanor, and if
the gossip racing through London was to be
believed, she would never be fully accepted
again. So Robert dithered and tried to avoid
her by cancelling many of his engagements and
telling himself he had been neglecting his
cronies for too long. After an exciting race week
at Newmarket, he realized he was cured of his
infatuation, for he did not think of the lady
above two or three times a day. He was a little
ashamed to feel so relieved now that Lady
Montgomery had told him he could not pay his
addresses to Kathleen earlier.

Tony and George, not knowing any better,
accepted their sister's reassurance that all
would be well and set out to conquer London.
They were not seen by Kathleen or her grandmother for some time, much to the dismay of
Kathleen's young lady friends who had hoped
for an introduction at least.

Although Lady Montgomery had been slightly mollified to find out that all London did not intend to ostracize Kathleen as a result of her folly . . . God bless the Beau, he had turned the tables neatly there by being so amused by the whole event . . . nonetheless she was relieved to find among her friends and acquaintances a few ladies who dismissed the whole incident lightly. In fact, old Lady Winslow actually chuckled with glee over the story and reminded Lady Montgomery of her own curricle race to Brighton more years ago than either lady liked to admit to.

"Have no fear, Eleanor," Lady Winslow said, "no one will think a thing of it in a few days. It is too bad we cannot manufacture a new scandal to take their minds off your granddaughter, but it will soon be forgotten in any case. I wish I could have seen her, though, I understand she looked magnificent, and several young ladies envied her her escort. Her brothers, I suppose? You should cultivate 'em, they set her off!"

This, however, Lady Montgomery was not prepared to do. Tony and George were allowed to go their own way in London, and had a fine time doing it. They were present one evening at a masquerade that Kathleen attended, and she was very glad to see them, although she took them to task for not visiting her more often. She missed them sorely, they did not criticize her as others did, and she was getting a little weary of holding up her head and

pretending nothing was wrong when she could
hear the whispers and see the pointing fingers.

The boys protested. They were only at the
party because a new friend had insisted they
come, but dance with her they would not. They
wore no costumes nor even a domino, for as
Tony pointed out, it was impossible to deceive
anyone. Even if they powdered their fiery hair,
their height gave them away every time.

Kathleen did wear a costume, not that she
thought herself disguised either. Her grandmother had decreed that she come as Diana,
goddess of the hunt. It was a flattering gown of
white, on vaguely Grecian lines, and the Beau
had suggested it.

"Always attack, m'lady! No hovering on the
sidelines trying to be effacing! Let all the
world see the Lady Kathleen as Diana, and the
gossip is as good as gone. Once they see *you*
approve, their guns will be spiked."

Kathleen also wore a laurel wreath on her
long red hair and daringly carried a small gold
riding crop to match her gold sandals. Lord
Ramsdale was enchanted as he made his bow.

"M'lady, as Diana you are breathtaking!"

Kathleen laughed uneasily. "M'lord!" she
protested, "you embarrass me! You are not
supposed to guess who I am." She touched her
diamanté mask lightly. "I do not really see why
I have to wear this. Surely it is no mystery who
I am, from my height to my red hair!"

"Never red, m'lady!" Lord Ramsdale exclaimed. "I would call it flame instead. A man

might warm his hands if he were to touch it! I wish I might see you wear it thus more often, streaming down your back!"

Kathleen blushed and made to turn away in confusion. She knew that only in bed did ladies generally wear their hair so loosely. Ramsdale caught her hand.

"No, do not go! I know I should not speak to you so, but I cannot control myself any longer! You must know how much I adore you, and how much I long to possess you always!"

Kathleen felt breathless and a little afraid as she tried to free her hand.

"M'lord! Release me! You cannot mean what you say, and I am sure this is not correct . . ."

Lord Ramsdale interrupted her. "No, the correct thing would be for me to go to your grandmother and ask her permission to pay my addresses, but you are not so missish as to insist on the niceties, are you? A girl who rides a wild stallion astride would not be so poor-spirited when a man who is wild with love for her tells her so!"

Kathleen stiffened and her eyes flashed.

"I do not desire to make a scene, m'lord, but if you do not let me go immediately, I will! You are offensive! If you think you can treat me badly because I have not behaved as I ought, you are mistaken!" She glanced quickly around the room for her brothers, but they were not in sight.

Lord Ramsdale tightened his grasp and spoke more softly.

"My love, I did not do it to insult you. I beg
your forgiveness, but I cannot believe you are
indifferent to me." A dangerous note crept
into that soft, insinuating voice. "Allow me to
warn you, however, that one way or the other,
I will have you."

He released her hand finally and bowed to
her.

"Remember, my dear, what I have said. I do
not play games, and I do not like to be disappointed, and if you do not love me now, after
our wedding I am sure I can teach you to
return my love. Yes," he continued as he let
his eyes wander from her flushed face to her
heaving bosom, "I can teach you *many* things.
I quite look forward to it, so do not make me
wait too long."

With this, he bowed ironically to her again
and left her. Kathleen was aware that people
were staring at her, and made an effort to
control herself. How dare he speak to her so!
Even as she thought that, she realized that she
was in part at fault. By flirting with Lord
Ramsdale to gain the duke's attention she had
gone too far, for although she had seen the way
he looked at her with desire, she had imagined
she could control him. Her head was in a whirl
as she sought her grandmother's side. She
would have to stay away from Lord Ramsdale . . . indefinitely! What did he mean, he
would have her, one way or the other! Surely
he had proposed marriage . . .

Giles stood across the room in a scarlet

domino. He had watched the entire episode and could almost guess exactly what had been said, from Ramsdale's impassioned face to Kathleen's blushes. So, my girl, he thought to himself, you have bitten off more than you can chew, haven't you? He was surprised to find that he had almost gone to her rescue, and was more than slightly angered that John Ramsdale had dared to touch her. He tried to shrug. What was she to him after all but a silly chit who didn't behave with propriety! He put his glass down and moved to Lady Montgomery's chair.

Kathleen was settling her skirts when he made his bow. She looked up, and the expression of confusion and unhappiness still on her face made his heart behave oddly for a moment. He spent a few minutes discussing the masquerade with Lady Montgomery, ignoring Kathleen in his confusion. Was it possible he was in love with her? The idea stunned him! His aloofness made Kathleen feel even more unhappy, and after he was called away by a friend, she asked her grandmother if they could possibly go home.

Lady Montgomery cast a shrewd eye at her granddaughter. She had not seen the exchange with Lord Ramsdale, and thought the unshed tears in that tight little voice were because Giles had been treating her so coolly since her ride on Diablo. Whether Kathleen knew it or not, she was in love with Giles, and Lady Montgomery rejoiced. Now she merely had to move the other part of the puzzle into place! Not an easy job at the moment, but one she would tackle with relish. Now, however, she merely patted Kathleen's hand and said,

"Have you the headache, m'love? Well, we will go shortly, but it would not do to retire as soon as the duke leaves your side. People would wonder. Let us stroll about for a while, and then we will call for our carriage."

Kathleen was suddenly aware that she did indeed have the headache, as well as a large lump in her throat, and that what she really wanted to do was to go home and cry her eyes out, but she smiled and complied, her back straight and her head high.

When her grandmother finally decided it would be all right to leave, she ached with the effort to appear casual and correct. She had stared right through Lord Ramsdale as he lifted his glass to toast her from across the room, and she was so miserable she dismissed Clara as soon as she was undressed, and would not allow her to brush her hair. In bed at last, she cried a little as she tried to see her way out of this entanglement. It was a long time before she slept, and the duke and Lord Ramsdale were tangled in her dreams.

Had she but known it, both gentlemen were also thinking of her, too. Giles sat before the fire in his library in a brown study, and Lord Ramsdale had a distinctly nasty smile on his face as he wended his way to bed after a long session with the brandy decanter.

CHAPTER XI

(The Right Proposal Is Also Declined)

The next morning, Lady Montgomery was surprised as she rose from the breakfast table to receive a note from Lord Ramsdale. He begged her indulgence and asked for an appointment for that very afternoon. She pondered this missive for a long time before sending a short note in affirmation. Could it be that John Ramsdale was serious? She had heard of his many conquests, but they were generally married women or opera dancers; he had never shown any interest in any season's crop of debutantes. Since she most assuredly had other plans for Kathleen, perhaps it would be better to deter him from going any further with her, and so she set the hour of his interview at four o'clock, a time she knew Kathleen would be driving with friends.

Lord Ramsdale was punctual, and he presented her with a lovely bouquet as he bowed to her. Lady Montgomery realized with a sinking heart that her suspicions were correct, and steeled herself for an unpleasant half hour, even as she summoned Bright to bring refreshments and thanked Lord Ramsdale for his flowers.

At last the wine had been served, and Bright had bowed himself out the door, and the inconsequential chatter had to come to an end.

Lord Ramsdale wasted no more time. He was correct and formal as he asked permission to address Kathleen. Lady Montgomery waved her fan. She had already refused Robert Marlow and another equally besotted young man that season, but she knew John Ramsdale could not be handled so easily. He was no callow youth, and he was deadly serious.

"My dear Lord Ramsdale," she began, marshaling her forces, "this comes as a complete surprise! I was not aware that you were contemplating matrimony after all this time. Surely it has been many years since your wife died, and this is the first indication that I know of that you wished to be married again. I have always thought that the way of life you have pursued since her death was completely to your liking . . ."

She paused, and Lord Ramsdale intervened. Although her words had been polite, he was aware of the double-entendre, and it caused him to lose his patience a little.

"My dear Lady Montgomery, my 'way of life,' as you put it, will naturally change when Kathleen and I are married. Furthermore, although *your* lineage cannot be questioned, the Lady Kathleen's is not so nice, and there is no bride price to speak of, to put the matter plainly. You notice I do not require a dowry, and I am perfectly willing to overlook the Irish connection. Surely not many wealthy peers would be so generous!"

Lady Montgomery seemed to swell angrily. How dare he! *Her* granddaughter was good enough for anyone! She took a moment to control herself, taking a sip of wine.

"How very noble of you, to be sure, Lord Ramsdale!" she said coldly. "I have no idea what Kathleen's feelings may be in this matter, but for my part . . ."

Lord Ramsdale interrupted her smoothly. "Lady Kathleen's feelings at this moment are confused. She is very young, after all."

Lady Montgomery seized on this eagerly.

"Yes, perhaps too young to be thinking of marriage yet. Why, she has just come out! A mere eighteen years in her dish, and you are considerably older, are you not? I had looked forward to having my granddaughter with me for quite a while yet. Yes, now that I think about it, I really think it would be best if she waited some time before taking such a serious step. Besides, Lord Ramsdale, your reputation . . . it has come to my attention . . ."

Lady Montgomery, in confusion, seemed unable to finish her sentence. Lord Ramsdale smiled.

"Yes, I am aware that my reputation proceeds me, and not to my advantage. But surely my love for the Lady Kathleen would erase that. 'The love of a good woman, etc., etc.,' and you may be assured that I *do* love her."

She looked straight at him and saw the
eagerness in those cold eyes. What she saw was
not love. Handsome as he was, she could not
help but shudder. Even if she did not have her
heart set on Giles for Kathleen, she would not
give her to this devil of a man.

She rose abruptly and rang for Bright, termi-
nating the interview.

"I will need time to consider this, m'lord,"
she said politely but coldly. "It is not a step to
be taken lightly, especially since I stand guard-
ian here, in lieu of her father. I must also find
out Kathleen's wishes." She bowed slightly but
did not miss the sudden flare of anger on his
face.

He had no option but to rise and make his
bow in return.

"I hope you will not take too much time,
m'lady," he said. "I am not a patient man, as
I pointed out to the Lady Kathleen."

Lady Montgomery stiffened. "I will inform
you of my decision as soon as it is made. Show
m'lord out, Bright."

Bright held the door and wondered what had
occurred to make her ladyship so angry, although he had a very good idea. Lord Ramsdale was not generally welcome in this house,
and if this had been an interview to seek Lady
Kathleen's hand in marriage, he could only
applaud her refusal. Griffin, of course, would be
quite set down if her favorite were dismissed.

Lord Ramsdale strode down the steps, ignoring the butler. So! That was the way it was to be, was it? Lady Montgomery would see who held the best cards now, though. He had honorably proposed marriage, and he would not be deterred by an old biddy and her Irish granddaughter! Kathleen he would have, and in the end she would be glad to marry him. So wrapped up in his thoughts was he that he did not even see the duke and Robert Marlow strolling toward him, and brushed by them impatiently.

"Well!" Robert exclaimed. "Pretty cool way to behave, I must say!" He replaced the hat which he had removed in anticipation of greeting Lord Ramsdale. "I wonder what is the matter with him."

Giles looked thoughtful. "He appears to be in quite a passion, does he not? One can only hope it was some severe disappointment."

Robert chuckled. "I know what disappointment *I* would hope for. I hope, for her sake, the Lady Kathleen has sent him packing!"

The two cousins continued on their way to Brooks', and since Robert chatted gaily all the way, he did not notice Giles' preoccupation.

Kathleen and Lady Montgomery were both pleased to hear that evening that Lord Ramsdale had retired to the country again. Lady Montgomery had decided to say nothing to Kathleen about his proposal, and her granddaughter was relieved that she did not have to face him again. Now she merely had to face Giles Brentwood. He suddenly seemed to be everywhere. At every ball, every riding party, every rout she attended, she would be sure to see his tall form and dark head somewhere in the crowd, and he always paused to speak to her grandmother and her. He did not ask her to dance very often and never stayed by her side for very long, but she seemed to catch his eye whenever she looked in his direction. He almost appeared to be staring at her! It was confusing, and she began to wish he had been called out of town too. He had never completely lost the coolness engendered by her escapade with Diablo, and she still remembered his angry words and frown on that occasion. It made her self-conscious and stiff with him.

Lady Montgomery was aware of Giles' interest too, but she ignored it and appeared cool and casual with him, although inwardly she was exulting. If the truth be told, Giles himself was astonished by his actions. At the ripe age of six and twenty, to find himself caught by a tall young chit of a girl with bright red hair who treated him with indifference was a novelty he wasn't sure he liked.

So Giles brooded, Lady Montgomery was unfailingly polite but uninterested, and Kathleen tried to avoid him. And there matters might have rested if Giles had not asked her to dance one particular evening. She longed to refuse him, but rose obediently at her grandmother's urging, and proceeded him to the floor. Giles took her in his arms for the waltz, and suddenly he knew that this girl was the

one he had been waiting for all these years.
Never mind if she set society buzzing with her
escapades, never mind that with her Irish
background she was no match for the Duke of
Havenhall, never mind that he could not for
the life of him figure her out; this was the girl!
He tightened his arm around her waist and
gazed down at her with his heart in his eyes.
The added pressure of that strong arm caused
Kathleen to glance up at him, and her own
heart seemed to stop. Her step faltered, but
that just made Giles hold her closer.

"Kathleen!" he said compellingly, "I must
speak to you! I have waited all this time . . ."
He broke off in confusion at the anger in her
eyes. "What is it? Why do you look at me that
way?"

What she had seen in his eyes was only too
clear, and Kathleen was suddenly confused, for
she knew, in her heart, that she had always
loved him. Her desire to punish him for the
things he had said to Robert during their first
meeting had been merely a disguise of her real
feelings. It was upsetting to realize that her so-
called "revenge" had been nothing more than a
ruse to see him and try and make him love her
too. But now, after treating her so coldly for so
long, he thought he could just announce his
love, and she was supposed to . . . well! With
her head whirling, she pulled away from him
and tried to escape. Giles held her even more
tightly.

"No you don't, you little fool! Do you think

you are going to make us both look ridiculous
by tearing away from me in the middle of the
dance? Haven't you done enough to set society
buzzing without adding to your faults?" The
duke's mouth was tight with anger now too as
he continued the waltz automatically, and
Kathleen thought she would feel the pressure
of his hands all her life. Her feet followed the
steps obediently, but her anger rose as he
continued.

"I do not know what is the matter with you!
You really must stop having these scenes with
gentlemen in public!"

Thus Giles, accomplished and polished,
blurted out his frustration at the scene he had
witnessed her in with Lord Ramsdale. Kathleen
was now as white as he was.

"How dare you!" she hissed. "What right
have you to say these things to me?"

Giles smiled, but it was not a smile to warm
her heart.

"No right at all, m'lady, you are quite correct. However, it is courteous to at least listen
when a gentleman proposes marriage. Oh, yes,"
he continued as she gasped. "Yes, I was about
to propose marriage. I made the mistake of
thinking myself desperately in love with you, so
much in love, in fact, that I could not even
wait 'til we were alone, or speak to your grandmother first. You seem to attract this kind of
proposal, do you not? Well, my dear, you have
opened my eyes. You are nothing but an ill-
tempered virago, and I count myself fortunate

to have so narrowly escaped committing myself!"

"Fortunate, indeed, m'lord!" Kathleen interposed rapidly. "But you may rest assured
that your escape was not as narrow as you
feared. There is no power on earth that could
make me marry you. I loathe you, completely
loathe you! You are arrogant, opinionated,
proud, and conceited, and how dare you say
those things about me? 'Too tall, too mannish,
too gauche! Perfect for my setting.' Indeed!
Well, it gives me great pleasure to tell you that
you do not please me at all, and I do not
consider you perfect for *any* setting in which I
find myself!"

The dance ended just then, and Giles had no
chance to reply to this impassioned speech, the
end of which had completely confused him. He
bowed frigidly, she curtsied icily. Without another word, he escorted her to her grandmother,
bowed yet again, and left the room. Lady
Montgomery was agog; Kathleen was practically shooting off sparks, but she steadied her
breathing and smiled at her next partner, so
her grandmother had to control her curiosity.
She noted that Giles left the hall immediately.

In the carriage on the way home, she tried to
question Kathleen, but it was no use. The girl
seemed to be encased in a block of ice, and
beyond saying that she and the duke had a
disagreement, would say no more.

Kathleen spent the night tossing and turning
and crying. She thought of all the cutting

things she hadn't had time to utter, and then she wondered what would have happened if she had accepted him. She cursed him roundly one moment, and the next found herself wondering how his mouth would feel in a kiss. And as the dawn slowly lightened her windows, she wondered what on earth she was going to do next. Perhaps the best thing would be to go home to Ireland, but she did not know how she could bear to leave him. At last, exhausted, she slept.

CHAPTER XII

(A Visit to the Country—A Dastardly Plot)

When Kathleen awoke late the following morning and had had her chocolate and been dressed by Clara, she went down the wide stairway directly to the silver salver where the notes and cards left that morning were lying. There was a short note for her from the Beau, congratulating her on her costume at the masquerade, and although it was as charming and witty as ever, it did not brighten her expression. There was nothing from the duke, neither a note nor flowers. Surely he was sorry, as she was, for their angry words last evening, but there was nothing. She sighed, and Bright wondered what was amiss now. She looked so forlorn standing there, turning over the cards and notes. All day she was distracted and uncommunicative, and Lady Montgomery decided to waste no time in finding out what was wrong. She sat down and wrote Giles a short note, asking him to call the following morning. Perhaps she was rushing her fences, but it had all the appearance of a lovers' quarrel, and she was determined to set things right. Kathleen was engaged to stroll with friends that morn-

ing, so there was no danger of their meeting
face to face.

Giles was punctual. He bowed correctly but
refused a seat, preferring to lounge against the
mantel. He did not look as if he had been
sleeping well, and there was a slight frown on
his handsome face. Lady Montgomery was
blunt.

"Now, Giles," she began abruptly, "what is
the matter with Kathleen? She returned home
from the Clark ball in some distress and when
I queried her about it, would only tell me that
you two had had a disagreement. What disagreement? I demand to know; I cannot have
Kathleen dragging around looking so unhappy
and miserable without knowing the reason!"

Giles' expression brightened somewhat, although he smiled sardonically.

"She is unhappy? Since she refused my
offer of marriage with every aspect of dislike,
I fail to see why she should be unhappy. She
told me in no uncertain terms that she loathed
me."

Lady Montgomery gasped and picked up her
salts.

"Oh, yes, m'lady. 'Loathed' was the word she
used. I really must tell you that although you
have turned her into quite a lady, her method
of refusing proposals leaves much to be desired.
However, I count myself lucky in my escape.
Why I ever thought such a volatile, ill-tem-
pered chit would make a suitable Duchess of
Havenhall escapes me at the moment!"

Lady Montgomery fluttered her handkerchief and managed to drop her salts.

"Giles! Do not be foolish, I beg of you! If you came up to scratch at last, after all these years of avoiding matrimony, you must love her! And she loves you too, I can assure you of that!"

Giles' eyes narrowed. "What an unusual way she has of telling me that I am her beloved Giles, then, ma'am!"

Lady Montgomery snorted. "Of course she was angry and confused. You might have given her some indication of your feelings before you blurted them out—and on the dance floor too! What were you thinking of, Giles? And besides, she has spent all this time and effort making herself into a lady to pay you back; you cannot expect her to forget that so quickly!"

"Pay me back, ma'am? For what? I am all at sea, I assure you."

The duke abruptly took the seat opposite Lady Montgomery.

"You may not remember, Giles, but you made some statements about Kathleen to Robert Marlow while you were at Evelon Farm. Kathleen overheard those remarks; she heard Robert's compliments, and she heard you teasing him by saying she would never do in London, that she was too tall, too unfashionable, too mannish . . . well, of course she was indignant! So she came to me, determined to prove you wrong. She didn't think beyond the point of your kneeling adoringly at her feet, and her scorning you, and she certainly didn't realize she would fall in love with you, or what she would do when that happened."

Giles rose and began pacing the salon.

"If what you say is true, m'lady, it explains a great deal. Perhaps all is not lost, although at the moment what I would really like to do is turn the Lady Kathleen over my knee and . . ."

"Yes, yes!" Lady Montgomery interrupted. "Of course you are hurt and angry, but it would be fatal to continue to be the starched-up duke with her." Really, she thought to herself, men could be so stupid, even the best of them! "I am afraid any reconciliation must begin with you, and if you love her, you will surely see that."

Giles smiled and patted her hand. "Never fear, m'lady, I have some experience with angry females, I assure you, although not perhaps one with the famous Malloy temper."

He rose to leave, and Lady Montgomery felt immeasurably better as goodbyes were said. As he reached the door, he turned and raised one black eyebrow.

"One other point, m'lady. Can I take this to mean that you do not oppose my suit? One would be correct, you know, and not forget any of the little niceties . . ."

The door closed behind his laugh just as Lady Montgomery threw her salts at him.

He strolled away to his club, his heart lighter than it had been since the ball. A few squares away, Lady Kathleen was trying to appear interested in the conversation of her two friends. Why she had ever thought that Mary Ward and Beth Longworth were less insipid than the other debutantes, she would never know. Her heart was so heavy it was all she could do to inject a comment now and then as they discussed parties, fashion, and beaus. Suddenly, Mary leaned toward her and whispered,

"Kathleen, I think that seedy-looking man is following us. He has been behind us since we left the park, and he appears to be trying to get your attention."

Kathleen turned curiously, and when the man saw her looking his way, he hastened toward them, pulling his cap from his head as he came.

"Lady Kathleen Malloy?" he asked, looking straight at her. Kathleen drew herself up haughtily, he was so disreputable.

"I am she," she admitted.

"I have a note for you, your ladyship. The cove wot gives it to me sez it was urgent you get it."

"A note? I fail to understand why I should receive a note like this. I think you had better be about your business before I call the watch. You are annoying us!"

The man cringed away but persisted in holding out the note.

"Cor, m'lady, I means no 'arm! 'Twas just the big red'ead said you woz to get the note as soon as ever possible, it was urgent! Them's 'is exact words, m'lady, and 'andsomely did 'e pay me to find you!"

Kathleen interrupted. "A big redhead? Give me that note!"

Beth pulled her arm. "Oh, Kathleen, what could it be?"

Kathleen read the short note hastily. Yes, it was just as she feared. Tony was in trouble, and George had scribbled this note to get her help.

"It is my brother! He is hurt and he needs me! You there! Did the gentleman say where I was to go?"

"I'm to tyke you to 'im, if it please your ladyship. I've a carriage at the end of this street."

Beth pulled her arm again. "Oh, Kathleen, do you think you should? You don't know this man and . . ."

Kathleen disengaged herself hastily. "I only know my brother is hurt, and this is no time to be missish! Mary, do me the kindness of telling my grandmother that Tony has been hurt and I am going to him. She will understand. Tell her I will return as soon as possible or send word about my whereabouts. Please, this is important!"

Mary agreed, albeit reluctantly. Too late she thought one of them should have accompanied Kathleen, but by the time it occurred to her, Kathleen was already hurrying away with the man.

When they reached the end of the street, a

hackney was waiting and without waiting for help, she climbed in. As she ducked her head in the door frame, she saw another seedy man inside, and made to get out, but the messenger pushed her the rest of the way into the carriage and she fell in a heap on the seat. As she opened her mouth to scream for help, a vile-smelling cloth was pushed over her mouth and nostrils, and she collapsed in darkness. It was all over by the time the carriage began to move, and it was done so smoothly and quickly that not one of the passersby suspected a thing.

When she came to, her head ached and she felt stiff all over. She realized she had been tied and gagged, and there was little she could do to help herself. The bonds were tight and the gag efficient. Cautiously she opened her eyes a little and saw the man in the other corner of the carriage. He was fast asleep and snoring. She turned back to the dirty window. They had left London and appeared to be on a back road, certainly it was not the broad turnpike she and her grandmother had traveled from Hertfordshire. She had no idea how long she had been unconscious, but it seemed to be afternoon now, so they must have been traveling some time. The carriage was dirty and ill-sprung, and she ached with every jolting, since she was unable to brace herself. She put her head back and tried to think. Who could be kidnapping her? And how did they know about her brothers? That made it seem as if it had

not been done by men who were merely holding
her to ransom. Her eyes widened as somewhere
in her head she heard a soft voice saying, "one
way or the other, m'lady." Lord Ramsdale!
Could it be he? The carriage slowed and
turned into a drive. She could see that it was
overgrown and weedy, so she was obviously
being brought in a little-used back way. A
pounding on the roof awakened her companion,
and she hastily closed her eyes. Until she knew
more she would pretend to be unconscious. She
felt the carriage halt, and the driver get down,
and a moment later, the door open.

"Any trouble wif the gentry mort, Alf?"

"Never stirred the 'hole way, slept like a
baby, she did! Guess we'll 'ave to lug 'er in this
way. 'Ere, you tyke 'er feet, I've got 'er shoulders."

"Watch your 'ands there, Alfie! This 'ere
ain't for the likes of us!"

Alfie chuckled and grasped her under the
arms, and Kathleen tried not to shudder. She
felt herself being carried roughly up a shallow
flight of stairs and across what seemed to be a
terrace. A step up, and her right elbow caught
something solid.

"Careful, you fools!" a familiar voice exclaimed.

So, she was right! It *was* Lord Ramsdale! A
deep and bitter anger kept her still. Her cap-
tors carried her into the house and began
lowering her. Lord Ramsdale spoke again.

"No, not there! Take her upstairs and put

her on the bed in the room that has been prepared. Then come back here immediately!"

In spite of herself, Kathleen was relieved. She was carried up a long, winding flight of stairs and into a room, and then lowered, none too gently, onto a bed.

"Migawd . . . she is a beauty, ain't she?" One of them leaned over her, his sour breath preceding him. "Do you think 'is lordship would mind one cuddle, Alf? I've a mind to . . ."

"Nah, come on, now! Let's get our money and get out!"

She heard them thump across the carpet, and then the door shut. She allowed herself a shudder. So, now she knew it was Lord Ramsdale. This was obviously his country estate, or a place where he felt safe. It was within a day's ride of London, but where did all this knowledge get her? She was still tied and gagged and helpless. For a moment her spirits failed her, then she decided there was nothing to do but wait and see. There was certainly nothing else to be done, in any case.

Not too many moments passed before she heard leisurely footsteps approaching. The door opened, and she willed herself to be still. A figure came to the bed, and there was a soft, indrawn breath.

"Well, now, my beautiful goddess," Lord Ramsdale said silkily, "I can see the game was worth the candle. How very beautiful you are, to be sure! Allow me to loosen your bonds and remove the gag. One hopes those brutes did not handle you too roughly." He chuckled nastily to himself. "That will be *my* pleasure and privilege."

Kathleen remained limp as Lord Ramsdale deftly removed the ropes from her hands and ankles and untied the filthy rag from around her mouth. There was a pause, and then Kathleen felt a hand caressing her face and throat.

All the years of riding, all the muscles at her command went into a desperate leap upward, her fingers hooked into claws as she went for his eyes. For one moment she thought she would win, for she had caught him so by surprise, but her muscles were stiff from the rope and the jolting ride, and he was too strong for her. She did manage to rake one cheekbone with her nails before he pushed her back on the bed and held her easily in one large hand.

"So, beauty, you were awake after all," he said. "I am sorry that you had to be subjected to this treatment; hardly worthy of a goddess, was it? But I did warn you that I would have you in the end, did I not?" His free hand went to his face, and he frowned.

"And you have drawn first blood, have you not, madam? My congratulations." Kathleen stared up at him with loathing, her eyes almost black with anger and defiance.

"Unfortunately, the first rounds do not always tell the match," he continued. "I quite look forward to a little bloodletting myself!"

Kathleen frowned, and then realization and

a horrified expression crossed her face. Lord Ramsdale laughed out loud.

"What a pleasure it is to deal with an intelligent female, as well as a beautiful one. One so seldom finds the combination in a single woman. Now, my dear, I intend to release you. If you try to fight me again, I shall have to hurt you, rather badly I'm afraid, to teach you a lesson. That is not my plan, and it would be, shall we say, unpleasant for you. You cannot escape, and there is no one here to help you. My butler and his wife, the cook, are the only servants and they are elderly and rather deaf, so scream away e'er it pleases you. I shall find it extremely fatiguing, but please feel free to do so if you wish. Now, do you understand me? Answer me, please!"

His hands gripped her more tightly, until she thought she must cry out, so she nodded her head briefly. He would never hear Kathleen Malloy screaming!

She was released at once, and Lord Ramsdale rose from the bed and strolled to the windows to pull the drapes. She raised herself on one elbow, and when she saw him looking at her quizzically, hastened to sit up and put her feet on the floor. She was dizzy for a moment and felt dirty; other than that she was unhurt except for the soreness where the ropes had bitten into her ankles and wrists. As she rubbed them, Lord Ramsdale continued,

"There is water here for you to wash with, m'dear. Unfortunately I cannot provide a maid, but I am sure you can manage for yourself. There are clothes in the cupboards and closets . . . Oh, yes, my dear," he added at her look of surprise, "there is nothing you cannot teach me about ladies' needs. Do not look so mulish, I do not desire to sit down to dinner with a dirty, disheveled lady, goddess though she may be. If you do not change," he continued with a hateful smile, "it will be my pleasure to help you do so, forcibly if necessary. In fact, I quite look forward to it." He turned to the door. "I shall expect you in the drawing room in one hour, m'dear. That should give you ample time not only to change into something more suitable, but to reflect on your situation. Believe me, further resistance can only prove uncomfortable."

So saying, he blew her a kiss in mocking salute and left the room. She heard his footsteps going down the stairs, and only then took a deep breath. She put her hands to her forehead and for a moment was tempted to burst into tears, then all her training and a vast amount of anger came to her rescue, and she rose from the bed and began pacing back and forth to restore the circulation in her arms and legs. She went to the window, and as she had suspected, there was no escape there. It was a solid drop to the ground, two stories at least, and no convenient tree or drainpipe was near to support her weight. Disconsolately she turned to the room again. What she needed was a weapon, but there was not even a handy

poker by the fireplace. Curiously she inspected
the dresser. There were powders and perfumes
there, and a comb and brush in chased silver,
but no scissors or nail file.

She turned to the closet and as she opened
the doors, gasped in astonishment. Several
beautiful gowns hung there, as well as night-
gowns and negligees. She held a flame-colored
low-cut gown against herself and blushed.
There was not a great deal to it above the
waist, and what there was seemed to be trans-
parent. She wondered if Giles would like to see
her in such a *robe de chambre,* and then had
to hold onto the doorjamb as a wave of pain
went through her. Now Giles would never want
her. Their angry words seemed very small and
petty now; if only she had not argued with
him! If only she had not felt she had to repel
him because of her pride . . . pride! Even if she
managed to escape Lord Ramsdale this minute,
her reputation was ruined. A small sob escaped
her, and then her back stiffened. Even if she
were ruined, she would make Lord Ramsdale
pay for this, and surely sometime soon she
would get a chance to escape. She must be
alert.

He had said that if she did not change, he
would assist her forcibly, and she believed him.
Slowly she removed her stained walking dress
and washed with the water and soap provided.
Her hair was hopelessly tangled; how she
missed Clara now! She managed to brush it

fairly smooth and twist it in a knot, low on her neck.

She walked back to the closet to choose a gown. The most simple and modestly cut was of white silk, so she donned that and managed the hooks finally. At last she was ready and moved to the door. Better to meet him downstairs with the servants present than risk his appearance here with that huge bed dominating the room. Besides, she wanted a look at the house—especially the front door.

She descended the wide stairs slowly to a small hall. The door was directly ahead of her, and for a moment she was tempted to try for it, but she could hear voices very near, so she moved toward a lighted room directly off the hall. This did not seem to be Lord Ramsdale's principal seat; it was too small. Probably a hunting box, she thought as she entered the room, passing the elderly servant coming out bearing a tray. He bowed respectfully and stood aside to let her pass. Lord Ramsdale stood before the fire, impeccably attired in evening dress. He smiled sardonically at her as she approached.

"Somehow I knew you would choose that gown, m'dear," he said. "So virginal, is it not? It reminded me of a wedding dress when I chose it."

Kathleen blushed angrily, but he appeared not to notice.

"Come," he continued, "sit here before the fire. 'Tis a chill night, and the lodge is none too

warm. Allow me to pour you a glass of ratafia;
I am sure you could use it."

Kathleen moved obediently toward the fire
and seated herself with every degree of composure, although her heart was pounding in her
breast. She took the glass he offered and, after
sipping it carefully, put it on the small table to
her right. It appeared that she was to be
treated to a formal dinner party, with just the
two of them *tête-à-tête*; not that it mattered,
she thought drearily, if it were a prolonged
affair with several courses. No one would be
likely to seek her here. Her grandmother had
probably taken her at her word and was only
worried because Kathleen had not sent word
where she was, and how her brother was faring.
How long would it be before she suspected the
worst? And how long before she would be
found? Much, much too late. She realized that
her deliverance must come from herself alone,
and somehow that seemed to calm her agitation. She looked into the fire, not letting her
eyes dwell on the fireplace tools across from her
seat.

"Well, m'dear?" queried Lord Ramsdale, sitting across from her.

"Well, m'lord?" she replied. "The next move
appears to be yours."

He put back his head and laughed heartily.

"How I do admire you, Kathleen!" he exclaimed. "Here you are, in my clutches, as all
the worst melodramas put it, and you merely
look at me and say in that haughty way, 'well,

m'lord?' Yes, I *am* your lord, as you put it. Unfortunately for you, m'dear, you did not favor my suit, and your grandmother did not appear to favor it either when I went to her to ask permission to pay you my addresses."

Kathleen's eyes widened in surprise, but she only remarked as she smoothed her gown,

"Yes, but my grandmother has excellent taste."

Lord Ramsdale's eyes narrowed, and he made an involuntary move in her direction, only checking himself when she looked at him with hauteur. His voice hardened, and the cold blue eyes grew still more icy.

"I beg you to be careful, Kathleen. There are several ways that this situation might be resolved, and although they all come to the same conclusion, some of them are more pleasant than others. For you, m'dear, I mean."

There was a soft cough at the door, and they both turned to see the elderly butler standing there.

"Dinner is served, m'lord, m'lady," he intoned.

Lord Ramsdale rose and offered Kathleen his arm. "Shall we, dear girl? Perhaps a good dinner will brighten your outlook. You must be hungry after all these hours."

Kathleen was surprised she could rise so steadily and take his arm. Pressing her fingertips lightly with his other hand, he led her to the dining room and seated her to his right. It was an excellent meal, and Kathleen was horrified to find she was so hungry. She turned her wineglass over, to Lord Ramsdale's amusement, but she made a good meal. He finished the bottle of Burgundy himself, but it seemed to have no effect on him.

During the several courses, talk was necessarily desultory. Kathleen contributed very little, so conversation consisted of several anecdotes about the lodge, hunting to be had in the neighborhood, and the local squires. Kathleen was able to piece together from this a vague idea of where she was, and the direction she would have to take to reach London again. She was careful to ask no leading questions that would put Lord Ramsdale on his guard. The butler puttered around serving them, and mumbling to himself. Kathleen could expect no help there. At last he removed the covers and, placing a decanter of port before his master, and a dish of comfits and nuts near Kathleen, bowed himself out. Lord Ramsdale poured himself a glass and lounged back in his chair.

"And now to business, my dear bride," he said.

CHAPTER XIII

(Our Hero to the Rescue . . . Too Late)

True to their word, Mary and Beth hurried to Montgomery House as soon as Kathleen left them to go with the messenger. They found Lady Montgomery in the hall, about to depart for shopping, but when she heard their first disjointed sentences, she whisked them into the library and firmly shut the door.

"Now, m'dears, please be seated. I am very anxious to hear the news you have brought me, but I think it would be better if only one of you told me the story at a time. You, Mary, begin . . . but first, drat! My salts . . ." She rummaged through her reticule, finding not only the salts, but a large handkerchief and her vinaigrette as well. Thus fortified, she waved them to begin.

Mary sat on the edge of her chair and excitedly related the morning's events. In spite of several interruptions from Beth, the tale was soon told.

Lady Montgomery was frowning slightly as they reached the end, but she knew she should not alarm the girls. Lovely things, did just as they ought, and friends of Kathleen's they might be, but she did not want them spreading this tale until she got to the bottom of it.

"The note was from her brother, you say?" she inquired casually. Beth and Mary nodded their heads, their eyes wide in excitement.

"Well, my dears," Lady Montgomery said briskly, "I have been expecting those two devils to get into trouble this age! I never trust a man with that shade of red hair!"

Beth sighed. She had seen the twins and, although she couldn't tell them apart, would gladly have trusted either one of them if they would ever deign to notice her. Even her friendship with Kathleen had not brought more than a casual nod from Tony or George when they chanced to meet in the park.

Lady Montgomery prepared to rise. "I thank you both for coming directly to me. I am sure Kathleen will send word shortly. I suppose I shall be put to a great deal of trouble over this, and the sooner those two hellions go back to Ireland, the better it will be for all of us!"

Mary and Beth tittered and smiled, and felt immeasurably better. If Lady Montgomery took the mysterious messenger and Kathleen's abrupt flight so calmly, there seemed to be nothing to worry about. As Lady Montgomery escorted them to the door, she added lightly,

"I will have Kathleen tell you the whole story as soon as she returns, although we are engaged this afternoon. Perhaps she could call on you tomorrow? Until then, not a word! It shall be *our* secret, girls! Not that it matters what daring deeds her brothers get up to, but it would be better if Kathleen's name doesn't come into it!''

Both Mary and Beth agreed that they would be all eagerness to receive Kathleen on the morrow, and that not a word would pass their lips until then. Lady Montgomery saw them thankfully out the door, still chattering, and sincerely hoped they would confine their speculations to each other, for a few hours at least.

Bright bowed her out the door for her supposed shopping trip, and she proceeded to the waiting carriage. Although she did not appear perturbed, she had every intention of finding Giles as soon as might be and, with this in mind, directed her coachman to Bond Street where she hoped he might have gone after their interview that morning. It was too early for him to have gone to one of his clubs, so the chances were great that she might see him strolling along, as all London seemed to do, on this fashionable thoroughfare. Luckily, she did not have long to wait. She spied the duke standing with friends, in front of Hecton's Library, and ordered her coachman to hail him.

The duke took leave of his companions and joined Lady Montgomery by her carriage, politely bowing, but with a quizzical look in his eyes. Lady Montgomery showed her agitation now, in the way she twisted her gloves and whispered her news. Did Giles have any idea where the Malloy twins were staying? She felt she should join Kathleen as soon as possible, although heaven knew, at her age, she couldn't be expected to go chasing around London . . . Giles' brows drew together and his eyes narrowed.

"A message from her brother, m'lady? And one of them was hurt and requested Lady Kathleen to come to him?"

"Isn't that just what I've been saying? The two gels she was walking with came to bring me the news, and although I hope I have stopped their gossiping, I do not see how I can hold them in check for very long, and in the meantime, what on earth am I to do?"

Lady Montgomery began to look very perturbed, so Giles did not see any point in telling her that he had just observed Tony and George sparring at Mendoza's. They had attracted quite a crowd, they were so strong and so evenly matched. Since they had been stripped to their breeches, he knew that neither was injured or appeared to be in the least trouble whatsoever.

He patted Lady Montgomery's hand. "Ma'am, I have an idea where the Lady Kathleen is. Do you trust me as your agent in this? I have, after all, more than a passing interest in the outcome!"

Lady Montgomery sighed in relief. "Of course I trust you! Where are you going? Can I drop you anywhere?"

The duke shook his head and tried to smile reassuringly.

"No, thank you, m'lady," he said soothingly as he bowed in farewell. "I shall try to get word to you as soon as possible. In the meantime, try to appear unconcerned, and do just what you had planned to this day. If any inquire for the Lady Kathleen, perhaps a trifling indisposition? I am sure you will know what to say."

Leaving a vastly relieved lady to begin her shopping, Giles strode to Haven House, where he shut himself into the library and wrote several notes. He rang for his secretary as he signed his name to the last missive.

"Mark," he said as that young man hurried in, "do me the favor to get this note to Lady Montgomery's head groom Fitton as soon as you can. I am called away from town suddenly, so these notes should also be delivered this afternoon. I must cancel my appointment with Brummel, and oh, I almost forgot, my regrets to the Duchess of Kent . . . I am desolated to be unable to attend her rout this evening, etc., etc. . . . you know what to say."

Mark gathered up the notes. "When do you expect to return, m'lord? There is a riding party on Tuesday next."

"I think it is safe to say you will see me before a sennight, but do not accept any invitations until I return."

He turned to leave, and then added, "The note to Lady Montgomery should not be delivered until two this afternoon, and I prefer you take it to her personally, and attend her when she reads it."

Leaving a puzzled Mark Fleming behind him, he strode purposely through the hall and hurried up the broad stairs to his apartments. He did not summon his valet as he changed his town dress for riding clothes. As he was shrugging into his cord jacket, Brown entered with a pile of newly laundered neckcloths. He was amazed and indignant.

"Your Grace! Did you call for me?"

Giles looked up, frowning, from where he was pulling on his riding boots.

"No, Brown, I did not, but since you are here, perhaps you would put up a small cloak-bag with a change of clothes and my shaving gear. Do not add twelve of those neckcloths, if you please! And, yes, add my rain cloak to the gear; it will undoubtedly pour before this adventure is over!"

Brown stiffened. "Do I understand Your Grace? You will not be requiring my services?"

"Get on with it, man! I'm in a hurry!" Giles snapped at him. He turned his attention to a pistol he took from a drawer, and Brown hastened to get the cloak bag. He knew that tone!

Giles continued in a milder tone as he collected ammunition for the pistol. "You know, Brown, I am quite capable of dressing myself for one day. However, you shall pack a more extensive wardrobe, and bring it to Havenhall tomorrow."

He hurried from the room, followed a moment later by a flustered Brown and the cloak bag.

A few minutes later, the duke was attaching the bag and his rain gear to Diablo's saddle and exchanging a few words with an apprehensive Fitton, who was not at all sure he had done the right thing in loaning Diablo. Aye, and if it had been anyone but the duke of Havenhall, he wouldn't have done it!

Giles swung into the saddle and steadied the restive stallion.

"Good man, Fitton! Have no fear, the Lady Kathleen would heartily approve my riding Diablo in this instance!"

With that he wheeled the horse and trotted away. He headed for the north road out of town and, once clear of the villages on its outskirts, dug his heels in hard, and spoke to his mount.

"Now, Diablo! We will see how you will go for me. I hope you are as good an animal as you have been touted. I weigh a deal more than the Lady Kathleen, and we have a long way to go, but it is, after all, your mistress we ride to save!"

Giles knew he was taking a tremendous risk. From the moment that Lady Montgomery had spoken to him, he had been sure that Lord Ramsdale was behind it. He knew Kathleen had refused him, and he had seen his face leaving Montgomery House a few days ago. That would not deter a man like John Ramsdale! He was used to taking what he wanted, and Giles was sure he had taken Kathleen. But had he taken her to his hunting box? When Giles had rescued his cousin, he had found them there; would Ramsdale follow the same pattern? He was almost sure of it, and of course Ramsdale did not know that he was also in love with the Lady Kathleen, or that Lady Montgomery had spoken to him. He was probably feeling extremely safe at the moment. He would assume that the old lady would try to find Tony and George, and even if she did run them down, they would have no idea who could be behind this, or where to find him. By the time she figured out who it might be, it would be days too late. Giles' mouth tightened. He looked forward to the coming meeting with Lord Ramsdale. It would afford him a great deal of pleasure to deal with that damned scoundrel!

After an hour's hard riding, he was more than impressed with Diablo. There was no sign of fatigue, but he slowed the giant horse slightly. Diablo shook his head, but he dropped obediently to a canter.

"Good fellow!" Giles patted his neck. "We will stretch you again in a while, but we must pace ourselves. 'Tis only late afternoon now, and I know a couple of short cuts from here. With any luck, we should be at our destination tonight."

On through the golden afternoon they rode, 'til it turned to dusk. Giles pulled up at a small inn in an even smaller village and called for an ostler. As that man hurried from the back, he dismounted and handed him the reins.

"Rub down this horse, and then water him well," he ordered, striding to the inn. "We do not stay."

After a draft of home-brewed, and some bread and cheese, the duke leapt into the saddle again, and turned Diablo toward the road and the last part of their journey. He was confident he would reach Ramsdale's lodge within two hours. He prayed they would be in time, not, he thought grimly, that it would make any difference to Lord Ramsdale. *His* fate had already been decided, whatever the outcome.

In the candlelight, Kathleen looked back at Lord Ramsdale as steadily as she could.

"Business, m'lord? What business could *I* possibly have with *you?*"

Lord Ramsdale straightened in his chair, his face flushing at the disdainful tone she used, but he answered calmly enough.

"I think you know very well, m'lady. I did warn you, did I not, that I do not play games? By this time your reputation is quite, quite ruined. Your episode with the stallion pales in comparison. But comfort yourself that as Lady Ramsdale you will have a great deal more freedom than you enjoy now. You may ride your horse backward, e're it please you! And in a year or two, when our passion cools, I will have no objection to a paramour or two, as long as you are discreet. An occasional lover adds spice to a marriage, I've been told."

Kathleen lowered her eyes and tried not to shudder. Loathsome creature!

"Yes," he continued casually, pouring another glass of port, "you will be glad to wed me. However, I do not think there is any reason to refine on the timing. Wed we will be, I promise you, but in the meantime, here we are . . . together."

He smiled triumphantly and toasted her before he sipped his port.

"Surely my patience has been formidable up to now," he continued. "Shall we not try it any longer?"

Kathleen toyed with a sweetmeat on her plate. Her control was going fast. She was tired, nay, more than tired, exhausted, and she saw no way out of this dilemma. As she hesitated, Lord Ramsdale snuffed out a guttering candle. The house was very quiet. As he looked at her again with that eager passion in his eyes, she knew what she must do. She settled back in her chair and tried to appear relaxed.

"You are aware, m'lord, that I have five brothers? All very large and strong, and with large and strong tempers? I may be helpless now, but I assure you that they will eventually make you pay for any discourtesy you offer me now."

"Discourtesy!" he laughed. "My dear sweeting, such was not my wish. Passion such as mine is not discourteous; it is a mark of attention, if you will. And since they will not know of it 'til we are safely wed, what would the knowledge profit them? I have a special license in my pocket, and the wedding will take place tomorrow. Furthermore, I do not anticipate we will be seeing much of your family, unless you are especially desirous of going to Ireland on your bridal journey, and can convince *me* we should go. I had another destination in mind and, to be frank with you, would prefer to sever the Irish connection; it is unworthy of me."

Kathleen's lowered eyes flashed. How she hated this man!

"But discourtesy is out of the question unless you force me to it. I really do not want to bruise that lovely skin . . ."

Abruptly, he put down his wineglass and rose.

"The hour grows late, m'lady," he said mockingly. "Shall we retire?"

He drew out her chair, and as she rose she swayed toward the table. Afraid she was about to faint, he put one arm around her to steady her. Kathleen closed her eyes and tried to make herself go limp. As he felt her sinking toward the floor, he stooped to lift her in both arms, and quickly she grabbed the heavy silver candelabra and swung it at his unsuspecting head.

There was a distinct thud as the improvised weapon hit his temple. He seemed to grasp her more tightly for a moment, and she was afraid she had failed, but then his grip loosened, and he slid to the floor soundlessly, tearing the sleeve of her gown as he went.

Kathleen held the candelabra menacingly as she looked down at him.

Oh, dear. There was quite a lot of blood pouring from his forehead! Pray God, she had not killed him! He did not move, so she felt safe in replacing the candelabra on the table. Hastily she gathered up the napkins and a water goblet and knelt to try and staunch the wound.

A moment later she heard the front door flung open, and heavy booted footsteps in the hall. She turned anxiously. The duke stood at the entrance of the dining room and took in the scene dispassionately, a mighty frown disappearing from his face. She was speechless.

"I gather I am in time, m'lady," he said, in a normal tone of voice. He might have been discussing the odds at Newmarket, she thought fleetingly. He strode in, removing his riding gloves. "How very unkind of you to rob me of the satisfaction of dealing with the gentleman!"

He knelt beside her and examined Ramsdale as he continued.

"I might have surmised, however, that it would be so. That famous Malloy temper would not stand still for this type of predicament."

Kathleen gaped at him still, her hand dropping the napkin nervelessly.

"What, speechless for once, m'lady?" Giles smiled at her and took up the napkin. "I do not think you have quite killed him, unfortunately. What did you use?"

He looked around the room. "Ah, the candelabra! How careless of Ramsdale to leave that within your reach! He has certainly underestimated your ingenuity!"

Kathleen rose and grasped the back of the high-backed dining room chair for support.

"Your Grace!" she managed to get out. "How did you find me? Did my grandmother send you?"

"Your grandmother told me of the note from your brothers, and since I knew they were both well, having seen them shortly before she approached me, I suspected Lord Ramsdale's heavy hand in this. He brought another girl here once before, years ago, and I hoped he might follow the same pattern."

Giles rose and smiled down at her white face. He made no move to touch her, although he had been longing to take her in his arms and comfort her from the moment he walked through the door and had seen her torn gown and panic-stricken face. He did not know which emotion had been foremost in his mind; the desire to hold her close, or the almost insane rage he felt at John Ramsdale, but he wanted to give Kathleen time to recover, she had been through so much, so he continued with his bantering tone.

"I do not take it kindly, m'lady, to find Lord Ramsdale unconscious like this. I had quite a different fate in store for him, and at my hands too; certainly I did not intend for him to be downed at the hands of a red-haired slip of a girl!"

He was pleased to see that the remark brought some color back to her cheeks.

"Now," he continued, ringing the bell, "I think we had better apprise Lord Ramsdale's servants of what has happened, and then I think we might take our leave. I hope you have something more suitable to wear? It is quite a ride we have ahead of us, and I do not think white silk, even before it became torn and acquired bloodstains, would have been suitable."

Kathleen looked down at herself and frowned. She was still light-headed and confused. How had the duke found her so fast, and why did he speak to her in that light, teasing way? She gripped the chair more strongly still. Ah, she knew! Having seen her compromised in this way, he wanted nothing more to do with her. He had not forgotten her words of rejection, and now that recollection gave him the perfect excuse to bow out; no matter that he had arrived in time! She felt desolate, and suddenly thought she would burst into tears.

The old butler appeared at the door and hastened toward them, exclaiming to himself. The duke stopped him with a wave of his hand.

"You, my good man, will attend to your master after we leave. I suggest a surgeon be called, although I am sure it is only a flesh wound, coupled with a slight concussion. In the meantime, you will bring writing materials, and then we desire two horses saddled. My dear Lord Ramsdale will have no objection to our borrowing the horses, I am sure," he added, as the old man seemed about to protest.

"I shall remain here with my dear friend until you have brought the horses to the front." He took out a large pistol from his coat pocket, and the old man shied away as he placed it readily to hand on the table.

"Lady Kathleen," he commanded, "I suggest you go and change. By the time you are ready we should be able to quit this place with no further delay. It is unworthy of our attendance, I am sure you will agree."

Kathleen could make no answer, but she nodded slightly, and gathering her skirts closely to her, sidled around the recumbent figure of her abductor, and went to the door.

Giles made sure she had a candle from the table at the foot of the stairs, and that she seemed able to manage for herself. He was proud of her; no faints, no hysterics, no screams and protests of innocence. What a marvelous duchess she will make, he thought, his admiration growing as he watched her make her way up the stairs, without hanging on to the banister too obviously. He only hoped she was up to the night's ride they still had before them.

As she disappeared from sight, he went back to the dining room. Ramsdale still lay senseless on the floor, but the bleeding appeared to have stopped. Giles poured himself a glass of the gentleman's excellent port and seated himself.

The old butler shuffled in with a quill, ink, and writing material, and placed them before him.

"M'lord," he said in a quavering voice, eyeing the pistol, "there is only Lord Ramsdale's horse in the stable."

Giles frowned. Diablo, although not by any means spent, should really have been rested. Well, there was no help for it, and he was sure Ramsdale's horse would be able to carry them double if need be. Ramsdale was almost up to his weight and would be sure to have a sturdy horse.

"Very well," he told the servant. "Saddle Lord Ramsdale's horse. I will explain to him why it is necessary to borrow it in this note I am leaving for him. And do not look so nervous, my good man! I have no intention of shooting *you*."

The butler hastened from the room, and Giles drew the writing materials to him and began his note, a mocking smile on his face.

"Ramsdale," he wrote abruptly, "I cannot tell you how desolated I was to arrive and find you so indisposed, and by the lady's hand, too! I had such great hopes of dealing with you myself; perhaps more finally that I dealt with you last time we met here. However, I shall look forward to your recovery and our next meeting with great anticipation. By the time

the duchess and I have returned from our
wedding trip, you should be restored to health,
if you are still in England. I must tell you in
all honesty, however, that I do not think it
would be beneficial to your health to remain.
Since Napoleon has closed Europe, may I suggest the colonies? Surely there is enough action
there for a man of your scope and imagina-
tion!"

He signed it with a flourish and then paused
and added a postscript.

"Your horse shall be returned from
Havenhall as soon as possible. I do not foresee
your needing it immediately, the lady having
such a strong right arm."

He placed the note in a prominent position
on the table and rose, taking the pistol with
him. As he strolled to the hall, Kathleen came
down the stairs. Unfortunately, Lord Ramsdale
had not thought to provide her with a habit,
and she had been quite at a loss as to what she
should wear. The evening gowns were of no use
to her, and she had eyed her dirty walking
dress distastefully. How could she ride astride
in that narrow skirt? She inspected the other
bedchambers quickly and discovered Lord
Ramsdale's clothes next door. Pushing through
the closet, she had gathered up a shirt,
breeches, and a riding coat. Of course they
were miles too big, but at least she could ride
in them. She fastened her belt tightly under
her breasts to hold up the breeches, and realized she would have to wear her walking

boots with them. With the stock of the shirt tied shakily, and the hastily shrugged into jacket coming halfway to her knees, she was a ludicrous sight as she came down the stairs to Giles, and he had trouble hiding a smile.

"Just in time, m'lady," he said, taking her arm and leading her to the door. "Although not quite up to your usual style of elegance!"

Kathleen glanced down at herself. At another time she would have burst out laughing, but now she only said, in a small voice, "There was nothing suitable in the clothes he brought for me. I do not think he had riding in mind for one of my activities."

Giles frowned as he opened the door. "Do me the favor of forgetting what Lord Ramsdale had in mind, Lady Kathleen. He need never concern you again, I give you my word."

The old butler had brought Lord Ramsdale's horse around, and Diablo whinnied as he caught sight of Kathleen. She stopped in surprise as she saw him.

"Why, Diablo!" she exclaimed, turning to the duke. "How did you get him, m'lord?"

"I felt if there were one horse in London capable of what I asked him to do this afternoon, it could only be Diablo. I had no trouble with Fitton, m'lady, and I think Diablo enjoyed riding to your rescue!"

Giles lifted her to Diablo's back.

"I think you had better ride him, m'lady. He has borne my weight for many hours, but if we go slowly and rest him often, he should be able to reach our destination with no ill effects."

Kathleen patted Diablo's neck fondly as the duke sprang into the saddle on Lord Ramsdale's horse. The old servant fell back and hastened in to his master as they rode down the avenue.

CHAPTER XIV

(The On Dit of the Year . . .
Had They But Known!)

Mark Fleming had had a busy morning, delivering the duke's notes of regrets and drafting a few of his own that Giles had forgotten in his hurry. Mark was curious but, being an invaluable secretary, did not question the duke's motives or destination; instead he followed directions implicitly. Two o'clock found him climbing the steps of Montgomery House, and hoping the lady was at home, since the duke had been so very explicit about the time. He did not want to have to seek her out.

Kathleen's grandmother was indeed at home. After finding Giles and telling him the whole, she had tried to follow her original plans for the day: shopping in the morning, and then a luncheon with her old friend Lady Winslow. As she left this lady's house and returned to her carriage, she realized that the strain of appearing perfectly normal when she was really quite perturbed was taking its toll. Where could the girl be? And could Giles find her? Suddenly she knew she must go home; perhaps Kathleen was there even now, or there might be a message from the duke. Since she had no interest whatsoever in the remainder of her afternoon calls, she so instructed her coachman.

She questioned Bright as he ushered her in to the hall.

"Are there any messages for me, Bright? And has Lady Kathleen returned?" she tried to ask casually.

"A few notes have been delivered since you left this morning, m'lady. I have not seen the Lady Kathleen."

Lady Montgomery sighed and then shrugged.

"Yes, she had probably gone on with friends, and it will be quite a while before I see her. Bring the notes to the library, if you please, Bright."

She entered this room and dropped her shawl and reticule on a chair. Bright brought the salver, and she tried not to appear too eager as she began to open the notes. Bright made up the fire, and then hesitated. There was something wrong, but Lady Montgomery obviously had no intention of confiding in him, so he asked impassively,

"Would your ladyship care for some refreshment? A glass of sherry, perhaps, or some tea?"

Lady Montgomery looked up from the notes. There had been nothing there but a few invitations, and suddenly she was very fearful. She had known in her heart there was something very wrong, all along, but Giles had been so matter of fact she had pushed her misgivings to the back of her mind. Now, with Giles gone and no message from him, and Kathleen's prolonged absence, she could not any longer deny her trepidation. Suddenly she looked very old and very tired, and Bright was concerned for her.

She sat up straighter in her chair and assayed a smile.

"Thank you, Bright. Yes, I will have a glass of sherry, I think. I have overdone this morning and I am not as young as I used to be! Some sherry will go very well."

Bright bowed and left the library. Lady Montgomery stared into the flames and wondered what she was to do now. She heard the front doorbell and started up, but she heard only masculine voices, and Bright would take care of it. He appeared a moment later.

"Your pardon, m'lady. A Mr. Mark Fleming has called. He says he is the Duke of Havenhall's secretary, and begs an audience."

Lady Montgomery felt quickly relieved, and her voice was stronger as she said,

"Show him in immediately, Bright! And two glasses of sherry, please!"

If Bright thought this was an unusual courtesy to extend to a mere secretary, he made no sign of it, bowing and fetching the gentleman.

Mark was with her in a moment. He greeted her politely and waited until Bright closed the double doors before speaking.

Lady Montgomery grew impatient. "Well, what is it, my good man? You have a message from the duke? Don't stand on ceremony, tell me!"

Mark bowed and handed her Giles' note. He

stood quietly as she read it, the only sound the snapping of a fireplace log. Suddenly she seemed to slip back in the chair, and her face became white and strained. He hurried to her side, and she whispered,

"My reticule! There on the chair! Open it . . . my salts . . ."

Mark hastened to comply. When she had her salts she seemed to recover slightly. She sat up and waved him to a seat, while she reread the note. As it dropped into her lap, she exclaimed quietly, as if to herself,

"Good God! What to do now?"

Suddenly she recalled Mark. "Are you in the duke's confidence in this matter, sir?" she asked, fixing him with a fierce stare.

"No, m'lady," Mark replied steadily, "I am not. The duke merely asked me to stay while you read the note."

The old lady seemed to be thinking pensively, so he added,

"I would be glad to undertake any commission that might be of help to your ladyship."

At this point, Bright interrupted with the sherry, and after Lady Montgomery had a sip she seemed to compose herself.

"I thank you sir, but the duke has been quite explicit in his instructions to me, and I suppose I had better follow them to the letter. I am to go to Havenhall today."

Lady Montgomery appeared quite bewildered in spite of these rallying words, so Mark said, "Allow me to order the duke's carriage, m'lady. I am sure he would wish you to travel in it. What time would you like it to call?"

Lady Montgomery pulled herself together and said,

"Thank you, Mr. Fleming, most kind! I think my maid and I will be ready in an hour."

Mark bowed, and took his leave. The front door had hardly closed before Lady Montgomery was hurrying up the stairs calling for Griffin and Clara, a million details whirling in her mind.

No words were spoken between Giles and Kathleen as they pressed forward in the darkness. There was little opportunity to ride abreast in any case, since they rode across country much of the time, and Kathleen was having all she could do to stay alert and keep her seat. Diablo stumbled once or twice, and she felt the duke close beside her. He led the way as if he could see in the dark, but she was still too emotionally upset to even ask where they were going. If Giles was taking her there, it would be all right.

After about an hour's ride, they passed through a small village and took a turning off the main road. Diablo stumbled again, badly, and Giles said suddenly as he grasped her bridle,

"M'lady, there is a small barn ahead. I think it would be best to stop awhile and rest Diablo. Here, this is where we turn into the field."

Leading her horse, he guided them to the barn. Kathleen slumped in the saddle, too tired to dismount, until she felt his strong hands reaching up for her, then she slid into his arms. She leaned against him weakly for a moment but then, recalling his rejection, made an effort to stand alone. The duke would have none of it and kept one arm around her until they gained the shelter of the barn. There he lowered her gently to a pile of hay and said softly,

"Rest here; I will water the horses and be back shortly."

Kathleen needed no urging. She was asleep before he gathered the bridles and walked the horses to a small stream nearby.

He let her sleep for perhaps half an hour and then, judging the time by the sky, went to wake her.

"Kathleen! Wake up! It will soon be dawn and we must be going!"

She shook her head but, as his voice penetrated her sleep, rose and went to Diablo. The duke spoke again.

"Nay, m'lady. Diablo has had enough. We will ride double now and lead him behind us. Come, let me help you up. The horse is quite capable of carrying us both."

Kathleen allowed him to toss her up on Ramsdale's horse.

"Poor Diablo!" she said as her horse whinnied to her.

"Never fear, he will recover from this day's work, and be none the worse for it," the duke said rallyingly. "I have never seen a finer piece of horseflesh, and his heart is the biggest part of him! Ramsdale's horse is still fresh, and we only have an hour or so more to ride."

Kathleen shuddered at the name, and the duke, who had sprung into the saddle behind her, held her tightly as they started out. She tried to sit erect as she felt the duke's strong arms and broad chest so close to her, but her exhaustion was too great, and soon she leaned back against him and went to sleep.

Giles smiled down on her tenderly. He kept the horse at a gentle pace, thoroughly enjoying the sensation of having her in his arms. Softly, he kissed her hair, and murmured,

"Sleep, my darling. I have you safe now."

Eventually they reached the duke's estate without mishap. It was not long until dawn, and the duke kicked up the tired horse a bit as they entered a little-used farm gate. It was not his intention to attract attention at this point, not after all the trouble he had been to to bring her safe out of it. Not that it made any difference, he thought to himself as they rode up to the manor. She will be duchess here soon enough! But he did not want anything to hurt her, and since they were here now, as was Lady Montgomery, the adventure was safely concluded. No scandal would attach to his lady's name. He rode the horse, trailing a tired Diablo into the stable yard, and spoke softly to Kathleen.

"M'lady! Wake up! We have arrived at Havenhall, and your grandmother is waiting for you! I am going to dismount now—hold on until I can help you."

Kathleen obeyed without question. Grandmother here, she thought fuzzily. Before she could ponder it further, she was lifted off the horse, but not set on her feet as she expected. Giles carried her to the side door of the hall, and found it open as he had ordered. He did not hesitate but carried Kathleen up a long flight of stairs, and knocked softly at a door. It opened immediately, and Clara peeped out.

"Your Grace! M'lady!" she exclaimed. This was quite the most exciting thing that had ever happened to her in all her nineteen years, and the thought that the Lady Kathleen was depending on her caused her to swell with pride.

The duke brushed past her and laid Kathleen on the bed. He glanced around, yes, all was well. Turning to the maid, he said,

"Take care of your mistress, girl. She will probably want to sleep through the morning, let her. Be sure she is warm enough, and oh, yes, get rid of those clothes! She is not to see them again!"

Clara bobbed a curtsy. Of course she would take care of her! The duke left abruptly, and Clara set to work undressing Kathleen and helping her into a warm nightgown. She wondered where she had found the funny men's clothing, but she asked no questions, and since Kathleen was half asleep, she did not offer any explanations. The only thing she said as she smiled sleepily up at Clara from the big bed, was,

"Oh, Clara, how good it is to see you again!"

The next morning, Lady Montgomery was sipping her chocolate when a note was delivered from the duke. She smiled with relief, as she read it, and then rang for Clara. Griffin was following them down to Havenhall today, with both ladies' clothing and trunks, and in no good humor, Lady Montgomery was sure. How she had bridled when she learned that Clara was to accompany her mistress! That lady had cut short any argument.

"Do as you're bid, Griffin! I shall expect you, with my carriage, tomorrow at Havenhall. Bring plenty of clothes for both Lady Kathleen and me; I do not know how long we will be staying."

The dresser sniffed, and Lady Montgomery continued,

"I rely on your judgment to choose the clothes, you see; that is something I could never trust the young gel with, although I am sure she can maid me for one day."

So Griffin had been slightly mollified, and only Clara was in the secret. As she went downstairs, Lady Montgomery thought it had all been managed extremely well. Trust Giles! He was all she had hoped for Kathleen, and she could not remember when she had felt so satisfied and relieved.

In the breakfast room she found her host cheerfully attacking a sideboard covered with dishes. He had managed a few hours' sleep, and now he was ravenous. He smiled at Lady Montgomery over a large plate of eggs, sirloin, and ham.

"Good morning, m'lady! A restful night I trust?"

Lady Montgomery smiled back. Giles looked

tired, but he was in his usual form. As if she had slept much on such a night! She remembered guiltily that she *had* dropped off more easily than she would have believed possible, but she only said,

"'Fore gad, Giles! Surely you are not going to eat all that!"

"Perhaps more, m'lady," Giles replied easily. "I missed my dinner last night, you know." Then as Lady Montgomery helped herself to a plate, and he poured them both coffee, he asked, "Have you seen the Lady Kathleen? I left orders she was not to be disturbed this morning. I think she will recover from this ordeal much faster if we let her sleep as long as she wishes."

Lady Montgomery said she had peeked in to make sure, as she put it, that Kathleen was really there, but thus reassured, had left her sleeping. Then she frowned and put down her fork.

"Giles," she said thoughtfully, "it is all very well to have rescued the girl, and no one the wiser, but what on earth are we going to do now? Surely everyone will wonder at us all disappearing from London, breaking engagements right and left, with no excuse!"

Giles raised his eyebrows.

"Wonder, m'lady? What Lady Montgomery and the duke of Havenhall choose to do? What impertinence!" His tone was definitely superior. "Surely our credit is good enough in society to do just as we please!" He dropped the bantering tone and continued, "I have sent a notice to the newspapers already, informing our acquaintance that the Lady Montgomery and her grand-daughter the Lady Kathleen Malloy are making a stay with the Duke of Havenhall . . . et cetera, et cetera. Of course they will speculate, but since I plan to follow that notice very shortly with an even more interesting announcement, they will not be in suspense long."

Lady Montgomery beamed at him.

"But of course! Your engagement notice, you mean! Then you found all in order . . . I mean, you were in time . . ." Her voice faltered, and the duke replied gently,

"All was well. I will take great pleasure in telling you the whole, with Kathleen's per-mission. You would have been proud of her, ma'am. Let me just say that when I arrived, she had contrived to rescue herself! I was merely her escort to Havenhall."

Lady Montgomery sighed in relief. If Kathleen was safe indeed, and there had been no duel to cause more gossip, it was better than she had hoped. Not that John Ramsdale didn't deserve to be shot, stabbed, or horsewhipped! She was intensely curious as to how Kathleen had man-aged it but resigned herself to speculation until Kathleen should wake.

That lady, in the meantime, slept on and on. When she finally opened her eyes it was after-noon, and Clara was unpacking her trunks and hanging her gowns in the cupboards. She brought tea, but Kathleen felt no urge to get up. She was still lying in bed listening to Clara's chatter and puzzling over events, when her grandmother swept in. For a moment she was soundly hugged and exclaimed over, and then Lady Montgomery dismissed the maid and took a seat near the bed.

"Well, girl, you are safe out of it, by what I can only term a miracle!" she began. Kathleen frowned at her sudden change of tone.

"What I mean is, how could you do such a ragtail thing? Going off with a strange man alone like that?"

Kathleen opened her mouth to answer, but Lady Montgomery continued imperiously. "Why did you not have the common sense to come home and seek my advice? Or get a maid to go with you? I was quite distracted; I am sure I have aged ten years this past day! If it were not for the duke, you would have been ruined!"

Kathleen again tried to intervene, but her grandmother was just warming up, and now that all was well, was feeling very put upon. She swept on.

"Aye, for even if you managed to escape Lord Ramsdale all by yourself (and I am most anxious to hear how you accomplished that, my love!), how would you have returned to London alone? We owe the duke a debt of gratitude that cannot be repaid. When I think of the vast amount of trouble we have both been forced to go to, it makes me feel quite undone!"

She stopped to use her handkerchief, and Kathleen finally had a chance to speak.

"I am so sorry, Grandmother, and I am so grateful to you both! I never thought of abduction or Lord Ramsdale, only of my brothers. But what happens now? Surely all London will be suspicious of our sudden flight to Havenhall!"

Lady Montgomery decided to leave well enough alone, although it had been on the tip of her tongue to tell Kathleen that Giles intended to make all right by marrying her.

"As to that, miss, *my* credit, and certainly the duke's, is good enough to carry it off. Giles has already sent a notice to the papers about our 'visit' here. And now, I think you should get up. Perhaps a walk before dinner would restore you."

She rang for Clara, and when the maid finally arrived, left the room chuckling to herself and mumbling, " 'Fore gad! The candelabra!"

Kathleen was dressed and sent to stroll about the duke's extensive gardens through the late afternoon. She sat beside an ornamental fountain for a while, and watched the carp. The duke had a beautiful garden, and at another time she would have loved to explore it, but now she only felt apathetic. It was as if she were numb, she seemed to have no feeling at all. She couldn't even bestir herself to wonder what she was going to do now. She had direly upset her grandmother, and after all that good lady had done for her! And Giles . . . suddenly her mind shied away from thinking of him. He had made it very clear last night that he felt himself well out of any entanglement with her.

If he loved her, surely he would not have been
so casual, so correct. She certainly had
dreamed that kiss and those soft words calling
her his darling; perhaps because she had
wanted to hear them so badly her mind had
played tricks on her. She sighed, and dabbled
her hand in the water, alarming the carp, and
continued to sit there sadly until a footman
came to fetch her to her grandmother.

As she was being dressed for dinner, she felt
suddenly shy. She had not seen the duke all
day, and it would be hard to meet him now. If
only she could have dinner in her room! She
suggested this to Lady Montgomery, but the
lady would have none of it.

" 'Pon my soul," she exclaimed. "You are
quite well, miss, and if you are still tired, you
may retire early. But to have dinner up here is
a signal sign of discourtesy to the duke. I shall
expect you downstairs by the first bell."

So saying, Lady Montgomery swept from the
room, resplendent in satin and plumes, and
Kathleen had no choice but to continue to
dress. She chose a gown of misty aquamarine.
It was a softer color than she usually wore, but
somehow she did not feel up to strong shades.
Clara chatted as she dressed her hair.

"Isn't this a grand place, m'lady? Almost a
castle! I quite lost my way this morning, it is
so large! And that Griffin! Her nose is so out
of joint she won't hardly speak to me! And all
because her ladyship brought me here instead
of her. Ha! But never fear, m'lady, your secret

is safe with me, which I don't think it would be with that Griffin! Oh, m'lady, it was so romantic the way the duke carried you up here! I was almost overcome, so like a fairy tale it was!"

Kathleen tried to smile at her. "Thank you, Clara, I know I can depend on you," she said, rising from the dressing table.

Clara beamed with pride. No harm would come to her young lady, not if she had anything to say about it!

At last Kathleen was ready, and there was no use delaying, for she heard the first dinner bell ringing. Clara showed her to the stairs, and she went slowly down to where a footman waited to escort her to the drawing room. As she entered, the duke rose from a sofa near the huge fireplace where he had been chatting with Lady Montgomery and came to greet her. She dropped him a curtsy, her eyes lowered, which was unfortunate. If she had looked at him she might have been reassured by the warmth of his expression. By the time she did look up, he had schooled his face to show nothing but polite concern for one of his guests. He had been too impetuous before; this time he was determined that nothing would go wrong.

"Good evening, Lady Kathleen," he said formally. "Won't you join us by the fire?"

She nodded slightly and took his arm, trying to smile as they joined her grandmother. Talk was casual, not only then but throughout the excellent dinner that was served by the butler

and several impressive footmen. During the
salmon with mustard and caper sauce, and the
mushroom fritters, she told Giles how much
she admired his gardens, and while the roast
duckling and the pheasant pate were presented, surrounded by tiny new peas from one of
the duke's succession houses, Lady Montgomery reminisced about Havenhall gardens of
yesteryear. The duke told Kathleen that Diablo
was fully recovered as they ate their crème
royale and various jellies, and suggested a walk
in the morning so she might see him for
herself. It was all quite formal, quite noncom-
mittal, and quite stilted. Kathleen felt she had
been sitting at Giles' left hand for hours, and
when the covers were finally removed, she rose
with alacrity at her grandmother's signal, leaving the duke to his port.

As the two ladies regained the drawing room,
Kathleen suddenly knew she could not continue like this. It was like acting in a play!
Why didn't someone mention Lord Ramsdale?
Was it all to be smoothed over as if it had
never happened? She knew she could not face
the duke again that evening, making conversation and uttering inanities until the tea tray
was brought in. She told her grandmother she
had the headache and wished to be excused.
Lady Montgomery eyed her shrewdly, noting
the flushed face and the eyes bright with inci-
pient tears, and agreed she might retire.

"I will make your excuses to the duke, Kathleen," she said as she kissed her granddaughter

good night. "Another good night's sleep will see you more the thing in the morning, I'm sure."

Kathleen hurried up the stairs and summoned Clara. When the maid arrived, she asked her to bring writing materials. She could not stay here and pretend any longer she didn't love the duke, so after she was undressed and made ready for bed, she sat down and wrote to her brothers, asking them to come to Havenhall and escort her back to Ireland. When her letter was finished and sealed, she felt some relief. She did not know how it was to be delivered, but Clara would help her, and the sooner she got away from the duke the better it would be. She was so calmed by this action, she fell into a deep dreamless sleep almost immediately.

CHAPTER XV

(The Path of True Love)

The next morning, Kathleen gave Clara the letter and asked if she would post it to London, for, as she explained carefully, she was concerned about her brothers and wished them to know where she was. Clara assured her there would be no difficulty.

"A footman rides up to London for the duke every day with a bag of instructions for the London staff, and any notes and mail there might be, m'lady," she said cheerfully. " 'Twill be no problem to give him your letter today."

Kathleen felt better; in fact now that she had taken some action, and after such a good night's sleep, she was almost her usual self. A footman brought her a note from the duke, accompanied by a lovely bouquet of flowers, requesting her to join him for a visit to the stables, and she was able to listen to Clara's enthusiasm over the flowers with hardly a qualm. He was a perfect host, she thought.

It was a beautiful day, and as they strolled through the grounds, the duke chatted casually of the estate. As they reached the stable yard, he sent a boy to bring Diablo out and told her as they waited,

"A marvelous horse, m'lady! I think I will have to return to Ireland and purchase more stock of his parentage!"

Before Kathleen could think of a reply, Diablo was led toward them. The duke ordered the stable boy to drop the bridle, and after a quick look of disbelief, he did as he was bid.

The huge black horse stood there, pawing the ground, until Kathleen called him.

"Diablo! Diablo!"

The horse whinnied and came to her, dropping his head so she could embrace him. The duke smiled. He decided to have Reynolds paint his duchess just that way, with the stallion. What a picture that would make, her hair like flame against his black coat! Kathleen became much more natural as they discussed her horse, until she remembered the other one.

"Umm . . . what did you do with Lord Ramsdale's horse, Your Grace?" she inquired shyly.

"The animal was returned to our dear, dear friend late yesterday. We did not harm him by pushing him the way we did," the duke replied with a scowl, and then changed the subject abruptly. He suggested a ride on Diablo tomorrow, and Kathleen agreed, her heart heavy. He obviously did not want to discuss Lord Ramsdale or her abduction any more than he had to, but she was not to know that he withheld comment because he wished to spare her. Instead, she assumed it was because the whole episode had given him a disgust of her.

When he returned her to her grandmother in the morning room, he went to join his agent, and was not seen for the rest of the day. Kathleen and Lady Montgomery whiled away the time with their needlepoint, a delicious luncheon of cheese souffle, tiny fresh biscuits, and fruit, and a tour of the house given by the duke's housekeeper. In the late afternoon, Lady Montgomery shooed her granddaughter to the gardens, saying she needed the air, and that she herself needed a rest before dinner. Kathleen strolled about as before, wondering if perhaps even now Tony and George were getting ready to come to her rescue. She had told them to find an inn nearby, and stay there until she could get in touch with them.

Dinner that evening was much the same as the night before, but Kathleen was in better control of herself now. She asked the duke casually about the surrounding countryside, under the guise of wishing to know more about where they would ride on the morrow, and learned there was only one village nearby that boasted an inn. The evening drew to an uneventful close with Kathleen pouring the tea in the drawing room.

The following morning after another bouquet arrived with her morning chocolate, she began to wonder if all the duke's guests were treated this way; surely he must have extensive gardens! She rose and, defiantly dressed in her black velvet habit, joined the duke at the stables. She thanked him shyly for the flowers as they waited for the horses to be led out. Giles caught her looking speculatively at his rangy bay.

"I know, m'lady, not in the same class as Diablo at all," he said. "But we will endeavor to keep up with you! Shall we have a race? Saying nothing about it to Lady Montgomery, of course!"

Kathleen smiled at him, her chin up. He had made no mention of her split skirt and gave her a hand up to Diablo's back with composure. They rode sedately from the yard, and she followed the duke to a track in the fields. Diablo seemed his old self, and only resented having to follow the duke's horse, but Kathleen controlled him firmly.

Soon they were cantering in the bright morning, and she felt her spirits lift. The rangy bay was keeping up as promised, so with a sideways glance at the duke, she kicked Diablo to a gallop. He needed no second urging and immediately pulled away. On and on they went, the bay hanging near her stirrup. At last she pulled up, breathless.

"You were right, m'lord, he has heart, but I still think Diablo would beat him in the long run!"

Giles agreed. "Oh, over a long course, no doubt about it, m'lady!" Then, as they approached a small stream, he said,

"Shall we dismount and rest awhile?"

Obediently, Kathleen halted Diablo and slid to the ground before Giles could help her dismount. He tied the horses to a nearby branch and strolled with her down to the brook.

"It is lovely here at Havenhall," Kathleen said, for some reason feeling very uneasy. "It is so good to be in the country again! I have quite missed Ireland, but I did not realize how much until now. London is amusing, and I have become accustomed to the noise and bustle, but the peace of the countryside is very dear to me."

Oh, dear, she thought to herself, I'm babbling!

Go right ahead, m'lady, the duke thought, I am perfectly content to wait until you run down!

Since there was no reply to these pleasantries, Kathleen continued breathlessly,

"Yes, I do not think I would care to live in the metropolis always."

She stole a look at Giles through her lashes, and what she saw stopped her conversation abruptly.

That gentleman smiled down at her tenderly.

"But there is no need for us to live always in London, my dear. I must often be at Havenhall, you know."

"I . . . I beg your pardon?" Kathleen asked, not sure she had heard correctly.

Giles took her hands lightly in both his large ones.

"Kathleen," he said quietly, "my last proposal was made impetuously, but you must know my regard for you is unchanged. It is my dearest wish that you do me the honor of becoming my wife."

Kathleen's heart was behaving alarmingly,

and she loosened her hands and turned away distracted.

"Your Grace! I cannot . . . I mean, I do not know what to say . . ."

Giles followed her, but he did not make any effort to touch her again. "Why, you might say, 'I thank you, Giles, I would be pleased!' "

"I cannot," Kathleen said once again. She was becoming much distressed. Of course she knew he was only proposing because he felt he had to repeat his previous offer, as a gentleman. If he truly loved her, why had he waited until now to tell her? How could any man, if he really loved a woman, be so formal and correct? Why didn't he kiss her and hold her close? This was not the way her dreams of this moment had always ended! She had never felt more miserable. She loved him so much, but marry him she could not, not when he considered proposing the "correct" thing to do! He had not compromised her, Lord Ramsdale had. Perhaps, she thought drearily, I should have married Ramsdale after all. At least he wanted me! She drew a steadying breath and turned to the duke.

"Your Grace, I thank you for your kind offer," she said with dignity, "but I find myself unable to accept it. I beg you to say no more of this, it distresses me."

Giles' eyebrows rose alarmingly, and he made a quick move to go to her before he checked himself. She had been frightened by Ramsdale; perhaps she still had not recovered from her adventure, but he had been unable to wait any longer. He saw a tear on her cheek and said encouragingly,

"Come, m'lady! We will say no more of it now, although I warn you I shall reopen the subject. I fear I was too precipitate once again. Shall we ride?"

He tossed her into the saddle, and nothing but commonplaces were said on the return. At the stables, Kathleen thanked him quickly for the ride and hurried to the house before he could offer to accompany her. When she reached her room, she found Clara doing some sewing, and asked her to go to the village and find out if perhaps her brothers had arrived. Clara was becoming suspicious, but Kathleen soothed her by saying she did not feel she could impose on the duke's hospitality by inviting them to stay at Havenhall, but that she did wish to see them. Reassured, Clara finally went away on the errand, leaving Kathleen to a sudden burst of tears.

When she had composed herself, she sat down at the escritoire and wrote two notes, not without ruining several sheets of hand-pressed paper and weeping a bit more before she was satisfied. She tucked them safely away and went to join her grandmother, who was strolling about the terrace admiring the Havenhall peacocks.

It was a very long day, but Kathleen managed to get through it finally, and even comported herself at dinner with dignity. The many courses did not seem so endless this evening, for she stole as many glances at the duke as she could manage without it becoming obvious. She would never see him again, and she wanted to remember him well; the strong, handsome face, the way his dark hair grew, and his expressive mouth. She lowered her eyes at last and asked to be excused shortly after dinner, leaving the duke with her grandmother. That lady was surprised at the fervent good-night hug and kiss she received, and was still adjusting her wig when Giles returned from escorting Kathleen to the stairs. He had been waiting for this opportunity.

"Well, m'lady, I have distressing news for you," he began. "I do not think you have been correct in your assessment of Kathleen's state of affection. I proposed to the lady again this morning, this time very correctly, and she informed me she could not accept me."

Lady Montgomery gasped. "*Could* not? Drat the girl, what nonsense is this? She is so in love with you she has been quite miserable. Did you not see the way she stared at you at dinner with her heart in her eyes? It is perfectly obvious that she adores you!"

Giles sighed. "If that is the case, ma'am, why does she keep refusing me? I do not think I am much more conceited than the next man, but I shall have no pride left at all after these numerous turn-downs! Perhaps I spoke too soon, she may still be smarting from Ramsdale's treatment of her . . ."

"Pooh!" Lady Montgomery exclaimed. "Did you kiss her?"

Giles reddened slightly. "No, m'lady, I did

not. I have just told you I was extremely correct."

"Well, no wonder!" the old lady cackled. "Why did you not show her you loved her? What gel wants a lot of high-flown words? You should have kissed her breathless, and then you'd see! Ramsdale, indeed! Women are not as fragile as you think, Giles, and Kathleen is as healthy as that horse of hers! She probably thinks you are proposing because it is the correct thing to do, with this stupid indifference you have shown her!" Men, she thought to herself. How helpless they are!

Giles reddened still more as he answered her.

"In that case, m'lady, and with your august approval, I shall . . . umm . . . how did you put it? . . . kiss her breathless at the next opportunity!"

They both laughed, the duke feeling immeasurably better, and ended the evening with a few hands of piquet.

Meanwhile, Kathleen had had the very good news from Clara that one of the footmen had seen both Tony and George at The Rooster's Crow in the neighboring village. As Clara was making her ready for bed, Kathleen yawned ostentatiously several times, and when her maid remarked it, said,

"I am unaccountably tired, it must have been my ride. Perhaps a good night's sleep will help. Clara, on no account are you to wake me in the morning. I shall ring when I want you."

Then, as Clara agreed, she added,

"Oh, before I forget it, there is some treatment

for Diablo that must be started early tomorrow. Wait while I write a note of instruction to the head groom."

Clara straightened the room while Kathleen dashed off a note informing the stable master that she wished Diablo saddled by six o'clock as she was desirous of an early ride. She sealed the note and gave it to an unsuspecting Clara to deliver.

After the maid had left, Kathleen laid out her clothes for the morning and packed her largest reticule and a bandbox with some bare essentials, then she lay down to try and get some rest. With any luck she would be far away before her absence was discovered, and the notes she planned to leave would discourage any pursuit. And since this was what she wanted, why then did the lady cry herself to sleep?

CHAPTER XVI

(Our Hero and Heroine Agree)

The spell of fine weather broke sometime during the night, and the morning was gray and misty. It promised rain later in the day, and Lady Montgomery stayed abed longer than was her usual custom. When she had leisurely drunk her chocolate, and summoned Griffin to dress her, she wondered what her activities were to be that day. She chuckled as Griffin dressed her hair. One of those activities was sure to be the planning of the most sumptuous wedding the polite world would ever have the privilege of seeing! She was sure the duke would waste no more time with her granddaughter, not after the instructions she had given him last evening. She decided that as soon as Kathleen made an appearance, she would suggest that the duke show her the family gallery. Not that portraits of long-dead Brentwoods were especially romantic, but it would be private, and certainly more romantic than being rained on in the garden or on the lake!

Giles was finishing breakfast as she entered the room, and they discussed the weather as she ate her toast and drank some coffee. The duke seemed to be in no hurry to join his agent or be about the estate this morning. He glanced surreptitiously at his watch as she told him of her plan involving the portrait gallery.

"I shall, of course, have something else to do, my dear Giles. Besides, I shall explain that I have seen them all before, time without number!" She smiled at him in conspiracy. "What o'clock is it? I fear I have been lazy this morning, but it was so gray I could not seem to bestir myself."

When Giles told her the hour was eleven, she exclaimed,

"Why, Kathleen is very late this morning too! Shall we ask her maid to wake her?"

Giles rose and rang for a footman. In a very few minutes, Clara appeared, bobbing anxiously to both Lady Montgomery and the duke, and wondering what was amiss now.

The duke took charge of the interrogation.

"Clara . . . that is your name, is it not? Have you seen your mistress this morning?"

Clara bobbed again. "No, m'lord, she has not called me, and last night she was that tired she told me on no account was I to awaken her 'til she rang."

The duke and Lady Montgomery exchanged glances, and he spoke again.

"Go to Lady Kathleen's room immediately. If she is asleep, do not disturb her, but come back here at once."

Clara curtsied once again and hastened from the breakfast room. Lady Montgomery looked at Giles anxiously.

"What is it, Giles? You suspect something, I know . . ."

"There is nothing to do, m'lady, until the maid returns. Can I give you another cup of coffee while we wait?"

Lady Montgomery refused, so he made himself sit down easily and chat of inconsequentials.

It was a white-faced Clara who returned to them, some several minutes later. She was so perturbed she forgot to curtsy, but neither the duke nor Lady Montgomery noticed. They rose to their feet, staring at her and the two notes she clutched in her hands.

"Your Grace! M'lady!" Clara gasped. "She is not there! I found these letters on her pillow, and some of her things are gone! Oh, dear, what has happened to her? I did not suspect anything last night, m'lady," she added anxiously to Lady Montgomery, "or surely, surely would I have told you of it!"

The duke grasped her arm firmly and extracted the notes from her grasp as he steered her to the door.

"Yes, yes, girl! No blame rests on you. Go and fetch Lady Montgomery's salts, and say not a word to anyone about this."

He shut the door behind her protestations and brought the notes to the table. Lady Montgomery had sunk weakly into her chair again, and now she said faintly,

"I do not think I have the stamina for all these alarums, Giles. I am much too old to put up with it! What can have happened now?" she wailed.

"And just when everything was going so well!"

The duke patted her shoulder and poured her some coffee before he handed her the note marked "Grandmother."

"Here, drink this up, ma'am," he said. "It will make you feel more the thing." Abruptly, he sat down and opened his note.

For a while there was silence in the breakfast room. The duke read quickly, his mouth tightening ominously. Lady Montgomery's note was longer, and when she had finished it, she groped for her handkerchief and sobbed,

"Oh, dear, the poor child! I had no idea . . ."

Giles plucked the note from her nerveless hand and read it.

> My Dearest Grandmother; My heart is very heavy as I write this to say good-bye. You have been always so very kind to me, ma'am, that there is nothing I could ever do to repay it, but I cannot stay. The duke has asked me to marry him again, and I know 'tis just that he feels he has to, to preserve my honor. He does not love me, and so I cannot bear to stay. Do not worry about me, I have gone with Tony and George. My love to Clara, it was not her fault, Grandmother, and my dearest love to you.
>
> Kathleen

As the duke finished this note, his expression brightened, and the only sound was Lady Montgomery sobbing into her handkerchief. Finally he shook off the brown study he had fallen into and spoke to her,

"Come, m'lady! There is nothing to be so upset about unless it is the muddle we seem to have made of this affair! If I had just followed my instincts, it would never have happened. 'Formal and correct!'—bah!"

Lady Montgomery looked up. "What did she say to you, Giles?"

He handed her his note.

"Nothing but a short thank-you for all my help and hospitality, as formal as I have been to her. I am glad I had the opportunity to see yours, or I would have been much discouraged. Now I know all is well, and where to find her."

"Oh, Giles," the old lady asked, "do you think she is going to Ireland? Will you ride after her immediately and bring her back?"

"No, ma'am, I most assuredly will not!" the duke snapped. "She is safe enough with her two brothers, and I have no intention of chasing after the Lady Kathleen in the rain. How many times," he added wearily, "must I gallop after the lady, do you suppose? No, having put us in this state, she can have a few days for reflection."

Lady Montgomery gaped at him. This was not the way the heroes of her favorite romances behaved.

The duke smiled at her. "Never fear, m'lady. I shall go after her soon, but I fear your plans for a spendid wedding must be discarded. I have no intention of riding to Ireland just to fetch her back to you; I have waited quite long enough, and the Lady Kathleen and I will be wed as soon as it can be arranged, and from her father's house."

The old lady bridled and looked so disappointed at the same time that Giles laughed out loud.

"Come now, m'lady! Think of the magnificent reception you can give us, when we return to town! I am sure you will outdo every hostess in London!"

This cheered Lady Montgomery considerably, and she put her head together with the duke and made several plans. It was agreed that she would stay at Havenhall until the duke sent word to her. Giles left her dreaming of flowers, music, champagne, and a ballroom redecorated in white brocade in honor of the bridal, while he made arrangements to ride to London on the morrow. There were a few matters to attend to before he pursued his reluctant bride.

It was several long, dreary days later that Kathleen arrived home. The weather had deteriorated to the point that she thought she would never see the sun again, but this so exactly fitted her mood that she took it in stride. Not so Tony and George! From the moment she had roused them at the inn and forced them to accompany her, they had complained vociferously of the fate that had taken them from London at the height of the season. First Kathleen had to

hear how George had been forced to cancel a
most flattering invitation to play cards with Lord
Dawson and his friends; then Tony chimed in
about a race meet to be held next week that he
had been most desirous of attending; then both
of them bemoaned an engagement at the theater
they would miss, until finally her famous Malloy
temper exploded. Neither Tony nor George had
ever seen her like this, wild with rage and at the
same time seemingly unaware of the tears
streaming down her cheeks. They went more
carefully from then on and, sure that something
was seriously wrong, did their best to smooth her
way through the rainy days, the inns with bad
food and damp sheets, and the inconvenience of
the crossing to Ireland.

At last they came to Evelon, and Kathleen
collapsed in her father's arms and wept. He was
alarmed, and when Kathleen saw how she had
discomposed him, she collected herself and tried
to make light of it.

"You know, Da," she said, hugging him again,
"I have missed you all so much, I could not imagine it! It is just that I am so glad to be home
again!"

Lord Malloy was somewhat reassured, and
when Katie Mary came downstairs to dinner in
one of her old gowns, with a smile and a kiss for
her young brothers, he put his concerns away. He
was not a very perceptive man.

Kathleen was on her best behavior, but sometimes in the days that followed she could not
help but think of the duke, and then her ex-

pression grew sad and withdrawn. Tony and
George had told their father of the sudden way
they had left England, and of Kathleen Mary's
mood, and he grew alarmed again, although she
said not a word about the matter. Thinking to
cheer her up, he mentioned having a large party
to mark her return, but she would have none of
it. When he pressed her with it, she said,

"Father, please let me be. I cannot be merry
just yet. I think I am overtired from the journey,
and the raking I did in London."

She smiled reassuringly, and no matter how
hard he questioned her, that was all the explanation she would give.

About a week after her return to the farm, a
large wagon rumbled up the drive, and Kathleen
was surprised to find that all her trunks had been
delivered from Havenhall and Montgomery
House. What did they think she was going to do
with fashionable London clothes on a horse
farm? She was glad to see her habits again,
though, as she unpacked the trunks with Mrs.
Keever. She had not felt comfortable in her old
breeches at all.

The housekeeper oohed and ahhed over the
gowns and accessories, so one evening to amuse
her father and the boys, she wore one of her most
fashionable gowns to dinner. Mrs. Keever helped
her dress her hair formally, but although her
family assured her she was prodigious elegant,
she did not feel it had been a success. The little
boys had been in awe of her, and the conversation was stilted, so she packed the beautiful

clothes away, keeping to hand only the plainest and most serviceable.

There was also a kind note from her grandmother, and she wept over it a little; not a word of reproach, just a fond letter to say how much she missed Kathleen and to hope the clothes arrived safely. She did mention the duke had returned to London on business, and Kathleen's heart sank. Not that she expected anything different, she told herself as she put her chin up, but still . . . The letter was signed with love, and Kathleen determined to answer it as soon as she felt more the thing.

Tom Gilroy was not long in putting in an appearance. He rode over one morning, ostensibly to see the earl about a boundary fence that needed repair, but he concluded that business in a hurry so he could meet Kathleen Mary as she rode in from her morning ride on Diablo. He straightened up from the fence where he had been leaning as she came down the avenue.

"Why, Tom!" she exclaimed as she dismounted, "how good to see you! How have you been while I was away?"

Tom blushed and dropped his cap. "Katie Mary!" he said, "sure and it's good to see you! I've been fine . . . No, I haven't! I've missed you like the devil! Oh, I beg pardon, but 'twas a long, dreary time you've been gone!"

Through this artless speech Kathleen watched him critically. He was just as large and handsome as she remembered, but now she wondered how she could ever have thought of marrying him, and that hurt her. Tom hadn't changed; she had. Would she ever be herself again? she thought, even as she chatted easily with him and coaxed him up to the house for some ale with her father. Because she felt so guilty about her changed feelings, she was especially pleasant with him, and he went off much encouraged. So much encouraged, in fact, that he called on Lord Malloy formally two days later to ask Kathleen's hand in marriage. The earl was delighted. Perhaps marriage was what Katie Mary needed, but when he told her about Tom's visit, she was horrified.

"Oh, Father!" she wailed, "I can't marry him! I can't marry anyone!" And with that she tore up the stairs and into her room and was seen no more that day. Her father was in such a quandary that he sought Mrs. Keever in the kitchens to ask that good woman's advice. He told her that Katie Mary had turned down Tom's offer, and what did she think of that? She nodded her head wisely.

"Och, and she'll never be having Tom Gilroy and his likes now!" she explained.

Lord Malloy frowned. "Because she has seen all the London swells, you mean? I wish I'd never let her go to London, and that's the truth of it, Mrs. Keever! Look how changed she is! And why is she so unhappy? Sometimes when she doesn't know I'm looking, I catch such a sad expression on her face, I want to hold her in my arms and soothe away the hurt, like I did when she was a bairn."

Mrs. Keever patted his hand. "'Tis my belief there's only one London beau she's interested in," she said. "I think our Katie Mary is in love, and somethin' went wrong. She says not a word, so I don't know what, but when we were unpackin' the trunks, she did let slip a name, and more than once too!"

He looked even more perturbed. "Aye, mayhap you're right, but if she's in love, and she's here and he's there, what can be done?"

Mrs. Keever shook her head. "There's naught to be done, sir! We must just wait and see, and be very patient with her. Mayhap she'll get over it in time, and all will be well."

Not for a minute did the housekeeper feel Kathleen Mary would get over it, but she had to say something to reassure the earl. He did look more himself at her words, and took himself off to the barns in a more cheerful frame of mind.

Some days later, he received an interesting letter from London. He spent a long time perusing it and then tucked it safely away. Although he mentioned the rest of the post to the family that night at dinner, he did not mention the creamy vellum envelope or the letter written on the hand-pressed paper inside, not the crest with which it had been sealed.

Next day he came down to breakfast dressed in his best riding coat and breeches, with his boots polished brightly. Kathleen and Michael were at the table, and they both teased him about his appearance, quite in the old way.

Michael wondered what handsome horse he was off to inspect, but Kathleen speculated that it must be a handsome widow at the very least, to call forth such sartorial splendor! He turned aside all their comments and conjecture.

"Never you mind, either of you! A little respect here, if you please, for your old father! I'm off to town on a matter of business and will not be back 'til late afternoon."

With that the young Malloys had to be content, and Kathleen soon rode out herself on Diablo. She was spending a lot of time riding him these days; sometimes she would ask Mrs. Keever to pack a sandwich for her, and be gone 'til quite late. She liked to be alone, where she did not have to pretend all the time, and if she cried a little, remembering happier times on these occasions, no one could see and question her.

This day, however, she had agreed to help Matthews in the stables, so she had a quick gallop and turned Diablo for home. Matthews was sure there was equine fever in some of the mares, and he wanted Kathleen's opinion. They checked the horses carefully, for this was a dangerous virus, and could spread rapidly. At the end, they decided to isolate only two of the mares and watch them carefully. Kathleen felt more cheerful as she prepared for dinner.

Lord Malloy had returned from the small town where they did the majority of their trading, and he was in a cheerful frame of mind at the table. He teased the boys, and Kathleen too, until the whole family was laughing. It was a pleasant evening, and after tea had been drunk, Kathleen prepared to go up to bed. As she took her candle from the table at the foot of the stairs, her father appeared from the book room and asked if she were planning to ride Diablo in the morning.

"Will the sun come up?" Kathleen smiled at him. "Da, you know I ride Diablo every day. Yes, I missed my long ride this morning, so I was thinking of asking Mrs. Keever for some sandwiches and planning a long ride."

"The weather will be fine, I'm sure," her father said. "Would you mind going round by way of Three-Mile-Brook, Katie Mary?"

"Not at all," she agreed promptly. "Is anything wrong there?"

He seemed to hesitate, and then he said,

"No, m'dear, 'tis just that I want that boundary fence checked. The Gilroys mentioned it, you know, and I want to be sure the men repaired it well."

As Kathleen agreed to see to it, he added,

"Why not plan to check it at noontime? 'Tis a bonny place to spend some time, as I remember."

Kathleen kissed him good night. "I'll be sure to check it, never fear, Father!"

The next morning was bright and sunny, and Kathleen and Diablo set off early with a large packet of sandwiches and fruit. They arrived at Three-Mile-Brook around eleven, and Kathleen

tethered Diablo near some lush grass while she
inspected the fence. It had been neatly repaired; her father would be pleased.

It was warm in the sun, so she took off her
riding hat and the heavy jacket to her habit
and, untying the sandwiches from the pommel,
decided to rest and eat here. Her father was
right, it was a pretty place. The water gurgled
over the stones into a small pool, and she could
see fingerling trout swimming there. She settled herself on a flat stone and watched them
as she ate, occasionally throwing them a bit of
bread. Overhead, small clouds sailed lazily in
the sky, and there was a slight breeze. She
sighed and leaned back more comfortably
against the boulders and closed her eyes. It was
so peaceful that she dropped asleep and only
woke at the sound of hoofbeats nearby. Diablo
raised his head and neighed, while she wondered who it could be. Not, she hoped, poor
Tom! She did not feel up to any impassioned
pleas of devotion, and she did not want to hurt
her old friend anymore.

The rider swung around a grove of willows
and pulled up his horse beside Diablo. The sun
was behind him, and for a minute she could
not see who it might be except he was tall and
as large as her brothers. She stood up suddenly, wondering if there were anything wrong at
the house, and then, as the man strode easily
over the grass toward her, realized it was the
Duke of Havenhall. She took an involuntary
step backward and gasped. She would have

stumbled into the brook for sure except that the duke had reached her and, without a word, caught her up in his arms. She stared at him, speechless, and he still said nothing, merely looking down at her intently for a moment before his arms tightened and he bent his black head to hers, blotting out the sun. His mouth was warm and alive on hers, and what began as a tender kiss soon deepened in passion, and although she felt faint and breathless, she didn't want him to stop. Her arms crept up around his neck, and he raised his head.

She caught her breath as she looked into those dark gray eyes, so full of a light she had never seen in them before. He smiled down at her tenderly, and then tilted up her chin and began kissing her again; her cheeks, her hair, her eyes, and finally her lips, trembling now. It seemed many moments passed before he allowed her to catch her breath again.

Finally the duke set her back on the ground, keeping one strong arm around her. Quietly, a small smile lingering on his face, he said,

"Breathless, m'lady? Well, I have carried out instructions, and it appears to have won the trick! My dearest Kathleen, I have the honor, for the *third* time, of asking you to be my wife, and let me inform you, m'lady, there is only one answer I will accept this time!"

Kathleen tried to compose herself, feeling flushed and agitated. She made as if to get away, but his strong arm held her to his side easily.

"No, no!" she finally exclaimed, her hands flat against his chest, "you don't want to marry me! You know you don't!"

"No, of course not," the duke said in an agreeable way, "but I have decided I must have Diablo and, in order to get my hands on him, will even go to the lengths of accepting you with him!"

He smiled down at her and again kissed her fiery hair.

"Idiot!" he said fondly. "Of course I want to marry you! Didn't I tell you so back in London, and again at Havenhall? You are prodigious hard to convince, my love!"

Kathleen's thoughts whirled around in her head.

"Yes, but the first time was before I said all those horrible things to you, and before Lord Ramsdale kidnapped me! You know you only asked me to marry you at Havenhall because my reputation was ruined!"

The duke sighed, and he said as he guided her to a flat boulder, "Well, there's thanks for you! And after I rode most of the day and night to insure your reputation was intact! Shall we sit down, my darling? I see this will take a while, not that it matters. It is a lovely afternoon, and I have you with me again—and there is no possibility that I will let you escape me one more time!" he added.

Somehow Kathleen found herself seated close beside him, her head resting on his shoulder, and both his arms close around her.

"I was a fool, Kathleen," he went on. "I felt that because I had startled you so much with my first proposal, that I had to be very formal and correct with the second. Your grandmother told me how far off the mark I was the evening before you left. She told me to stop talking, and to kiss you . . . like this!"

Once again Kathleen found herself being thoroughly kissed. She sighed. She hadn't known it would feel like this! From the top of her head to the soles of her feet she felt warm and tingly, as if her very bones were melting. Again her arms went around his neck, and she moved closer to him.

Giles took his mouth from hers a little way and said unevenly,

"Well, m'lady? What is your answer?"

"Yes, Your Grace, if you please, Your Grace," she whispered, although the dimple quivered beside her mouth.

He bent to kiss it, and then he put her from him slightly.

"Giles, not Your Grace," he said sternly. "Never anything but Giles from now on!"

Kathleen smiled up at him, her eyes slightly closed.

"Not even 'dearest,' or 'my darling'?" she asked innocently.

His laugh was unsteady. "Oh, yes, all of those, when we are private! And that reminds me, we have some business to attend to, much as I wish we could continue."

Kathleen smiled up at him mistily.

"Business, Giles?"

"I have a special license in my pocket, m'lady. Lord Ramsdale is not the only suitor of yours with initiative!"

She frowned at the name, and the duke laughed at her.

"You will wish to know, m'lady, that Lord Ramsdale has left England, quite suddenly. The on dit of the year, or will be until notice reaches London tomorrow of our wedding. Would you like to hear it?"

He drew a paper from his pocket and read it aloud to her.

" 'A marriage has been announced between the Lady Kathleen Mary Malloy and Giles Brentwood, Duke of Havenhall, Marquess of . . . et cetera, et cetera. The ceremony was held at the bride's home in Ireland and was attended only by immediate members of the family. After a bridal journey, the duke and duchess will be at home to friends at Haven House, London.' "

Kathleen put both hands to her face in surprise.

"Your Grace! . . . I mean Giles! You said this will be announced tomorrow? But when will this ceremony take place?"

Giles rose and set her carefully on her feet so he could check his watch.

"Well, my soon-to-be-duchess," he said, "I think Mrs. Keever has everything ready, Michael has fetched the clergy, and your father has managed to get all your brothers in their best clothes by now. We are the only ones who are not prepared, but since your grandmother sent several boxes, and the Montgomery lace veil, as well as Clara to assist you, we should not take long. Shall we not delay another minute?"

They strolled to their horses, arms entwined. As he put his arms around her to toss her into the saddle, he said firmly,

"I shall take great care that this is the last time I have to come tearing after you, my love. I find that no setting is 'perfect' unless you are there with me!"

Kathleen smiled up at him happily, and then stopped him with an urgent hand on his arm.

"Giles! Wait!" she exclaimed. "Who *was* Heliodora?"

The duke threw back his head and laughed.

"From the Greek, dearest," he explained, and then quoted,

> "*Heliodora, the red, red rose;*
> *The rose that lovers love!*"

And laughing together, they rode back to Evelon and the beginning.

THE END